NOCTURNE

"Lyrical, lush, and inter

THE SECRET DIARIES OF CHARLOTTE BRONTË
Audiobook Audie Award for Romance

"Syrie James takes the biography of Brontë and sketches it into a work of art." —*Sacramento Book Review*

THE LOST MEMOIRS OF JANE AUSTEN

"The reader pulls for the heroine and her dreams of love ... offers a deeper understanding of what Austen's life might have been like." —*The Los Angeles Times*

DRACULA, MY LOVE

"A spooky yet thoroughly romantic love story." —*Chicago Tribune*

THE MISSING MANUSCRIPT OF JANE AUSTEN

"A literary feast for Anglophiles." —*Publishers Weekly*

"This richly imagined Jane Austen 'road novel' is such a page turner!"—*Kirkus Reviews* (starred review)

FORBIDDEN

"If you enjoy angels, 'forbidden' romance and dashing heroes, this should be added to your TBR." —*USA Today*

JANE AUSTEN'S FIRST LOVE

"Truly riveting. James's latest will charm Austen fans as well as Austen unfamiliars ... Romance fans will root for Jane all the way." —*Library Journal*, Editor's Pick

ALSO BY SYRIE JAMES

FLOATING ON AIR

A STRUCK BY LOVE NOVEL

SYRIE JAMES

This book is a work of fiction. Names, characters, places, organizations, incidents, and dialogue are drawn from the the author's imagination and are not to be construed as real. Any resemblance to actual events or persons, living or dead, is entirely coincidental.

FLOATING ON AIR

Previously published as *Songbird.*

CHAPTER 1

Anaheim, California
June 1986

The song ended. Desiree leaned forward on the high stool, bringing her lips close to the microphone.

"That was Rita Coolidge singing the hit from her new album, 'Be Mine Tonight.' Before that we heard from Johnny Mathis with 'So in Love with You.'"

She checked the pie-sized clock on the wall above the console. "It's twenty-five past three here on this hot and sunny Wednesday afternoon in June. You're listening to KICK Anaheim, 102 on your FM dial. This is Desiree Germain keeping you company for that long drive home."

Right on cue, the first soft notes of the next song began to play. Desiree removed her headphones and lifted her long hair off her shoulders, letting the cool air from the overhead vent flow freely around her neck.

A fire-engine red bumper sticker affixed to the window above the console caught her eye: SPEND THE NIGHT WITH DESIREE ... KICK 102 FM!

Time for a new slogan, she thought, carefully peeling the length of vinyl off the glass and tossing it in the trash. Seven years of working evenings and nights, and she had finally made it: Prime time, daytime radio in Southern California.

So whatever you do, she told herself, don't blow it.

She turned up the volume control, leaned her head back, and closed her eyes, hoping the mellow tune's soothing rhythm would help calm her senses.

It's the same job as before, only the time has changed.

Forget about Arbitron and shares and rating points. Forget about the hundreds of would-be deejays standing in the wings, chomping at the bit, just waiting for you to mess up. Put it out of your mind.

You're good—one of the best jocks this station has—or Sam wouldn't have given you the afternoon drive. Just relax and enjoy yourself.

She heard the studio door open and straightened up. Tom, the station's part-time gofer, rushed in, his forehead perspiring beneath a tangle of wiry hair.

"Man, it's hot out there." He fanned his youthful face with a stack of small newsprint sheets. "The air conditioner can barely keep up. You're lucky. Your cubicle is nice and cool."

"I know. I am lucky. And *cubicle* is right." Desiree glanced about the tiny studio with a smile. Some people, she knew, got claustrophobic in elevators, yet she was stuck in this microscopic space for four hours straight every weekday.

She didn't mind. She didn't care, either, that the equipment was so outdated it was practically obsolete. Or the fact that the dingy beige walls were plastered with old, faded, dog-eared posters of Elvis, The Beatles, Kenny Rogers, and Streisand. She loved every last, musty detail of the place.

"Here's the latest, fresh off the wire." Tom handed her the stack of newsprint.

"Anything good?"

"What do you think this is, *Sixty Minutes?*"

Desiree leafed through the pile of news briefs, reading some of the titles aloud. "'New smoking control law giving people nicotine fits.' Cute, but no cigar. 'Laundromat owner taken to the cleaners in palimony suit.'" She sighed. "Why do we do these, anyway? We're not a news station."

"Don't ask me." Tom shrugged as he turned to leave. "Sam likes this kind of stuff. And one must never argue with the P.D." Before shutting the door, he turned back to her and mimicked their program director's gravelly voice. "Above all else—*Be Entertaining.*"

Desiree laughed as she slipped on her headphones. "I'll give it my best shot. Today's news can use all the help it can get."

A familiar refrain signaled the end of the song. She pushed the start button on the deck to the left of the console. A glance at the digital countdown timer told her she had fifteen seconds. Just then Tom pressed his face up against the glass of the window above the console, staring in at her with a goofy expression.

She smothered another laugh, dropping her voice an octave as she said into the mike, "If you're sitting in traffic right now, feeling that tension creeping up your spine, here's the perfect way to get rid of all that stress. Just imagine that I'm sitting next to you, giving your shoulders a nice, long, massage." She cringed. *Nice, long massage? Did I really just say that?*

The commercial break began. Desiree again plucked off her headphones and glanced up at Tom, who was mouthing the word "outrageous" at her as he walked away.

Outrageous. That's what the reporter from the Los Angeles Times had written about her in this morning's review of her new afternoon show. "One outrageous, sexy woman, whose luscious, lusty voice could, with one well-placed sigh, bring half the male population of Southern California to its knees."

She laughed softly to herself. Luscious? *Lusty?* Hardly. When it came to looks, she was nothing special. People said she was pretty, but she believed they were just being nice. In school, she'd never been a cheerleader or prom queen, and she hadn't dated much. She'd been friends with the geeks and bookworms, the less-than-popular crowd.

Pretty girls had blue eyes. Or green eyes. Or brown. Her eyes were amber. Kids used to tease her about it and call her Stoplight, a nickname that still hurt every time she recalled it. Who had amber eyes? Nobody.

Her hair wasn't much better. It fell past her shoulders in waves that were hard to tame, a nondescript brown blended with dark blond.

4

Somehow, though, her deep voice seemed to lead people to expect a tall, gorgeous, voluptuous bombshell. No way on earth could she ever hope to fit that image.

She was petite in every sense of the word. She possessed curves in all the right places, but no matter how long or how hard she'd wished for it, she had never quite reached the five-foot-three-inch mark.

Thirty years old, she had endured a lifetime of jokes about the discrepancy between her voice and her looks. She'd seen the disappointment in people's eyes too many times when they met her and discovered she wasn't the sex symbol they'd imagined.

Still, her voice was her biggest asset. Sam insisted that teasing banter meant higher ratings, and he had encouraged the on-air persona she'd adopted. The listeners couldn't see her, after all. Her name fit the image. What harm could there be in playing along?

Desiree scanned the news brief she'd selected, waiting for the commercial break to end, then threw the mike switch to program and turned up the volume.

"Here's an item of interest for all you soft drink guzzlers out there. Looks like the new diet drink, Sparkle Light, is losing steam. In an unexpected move yesterday, the parent corporation, privately owned, multimillion dollar Harrison Industries announced plans for Sparkle Light Bottling Company to go public." She went on to read the experts' analysis, which pointed a finger at a suspected drop in product sales.

"If you've always wanted to own stock in a soft drink company, this might be your big chance. But let's hope Sparkle Light picks up in a hurry, or you may find yourself making a big deposit, no-return investment on a warehouse full of pop without any fizz."

She played a groaning sound-effects tape. Next, grabbing a large pink index card from the board above her console, she announced it was time to play the Trivia Game. "I hope you're all next to your phones." She announced the number to call, adding, "I'll take caller number twelve."

All five lines on the multi-tap phone in her studio lit up with magical precision. Desiree smiled. The immediate response to contests on the afternoon drive never ceased to amaze her. This was the time of day to be on the air!

"The caller who can answer today's trivia question correctly will receive a complimentary dinner for two at Maximilian's in Huntington Beach." Desiree read a blurb about the restaurant, then punched the buttons on the phone one at a time, counting out loud and disconnecting each line in sequence.

"Hi, you're on the air," she said when she reached the twelfth caller. "Who's this?"

"Kyle Harrison." The voice was slightly obscured by faint background noise.

"Where are you from, Kyle?"

"Seattle."

"Seattle!" Desiree laughed. "KICK'S coverage must be even more widespread than I thought."

"Sorry to disappoint you. I'm in Southern California at the moment, crawling along on the San Diego freeway at the incredible speed of three miles per hour."

"A car-phone executive!" she announced with delight. "My first one on the air." Mobile phones were new and incredibly expensive. She found herself sitting up straight on the stool, conjuring a quick mental image of the man. A sixty-five-year-old corporate executive, wearing a pin-striped suit and built like Santa Claus. His voice was low, smooth, and deeply masculine.

"You've got a terrific radio voice, Kyle. Are you as good-looking as you sound?" she teased.

A split-second pause. Then, he replied curtly, "I don't know. Are you?"

Oh, God. Open mouth, insert foot. She glanced down at her worn, tight-fitting cutoffs and pink T-shirt. What kind of woman was he imagining? *Think fast. Be Entertaining.*

"Just let your imagination go wild. If only you could see the wicked little dress I've got on today. Electric-blue silk. Cut just off the shoulder. Terribly chic. And these silver spiked heels are positively sinful."

"I'll bet." He laughed suddenly, a deep, pleasant sound.

What a gorgeous laugh, she thought. She wasn't usually attracted to older men, but this man's voice and laugh set her spine tingling.

An inner voice warned, *Get to the trivia question. You've talked to him too long already.*

"Well, Kyle, I hope you can think trivia and drive at the same time, because—"

"Hold on," he interrupted. "I know this is a contest line, but I called for another reason. To comment on a news item that you gave about a company of mine a few minutes back. Sparkle Light."

She opened her mouth to reply, then froze. *Sparkle Light.* In a flash of belated understanding, she realized the significance of his name.

Kyle Harrison. Harrison Industries—the privately-owned parent corporation.

Desperately, she began to riffle through the stack of newsprint on her counter, her mind racing, trying to remember what she'd said about Sparkle Light. Something about a no-return investment, the product losing its fizz.

Had she sounded overly sarcastic? Defamatory? If only we had a seven-second delay system, she thought, so I could bleep out his comments if he starts to get nasty.

"The information you gave was essentially correct. Sparkle Light *is* going public. But the so-called expert analysis you read was completely off base. Since you popped up with your phone number so conveniently, I thought I'd call and set the record straight."

"Thank you, Mr. Harrison." She hoped her voice sounded as light and sparkling as his product. "We always welcome informed insights from the business world."

Why did she suddenly feel as if she had to call him mister? From now on, she told herself, I'm going to start screening calls. To hell with spontaneity!

"We're going public to raise capital for other investments. It's that simple. The move is no reflection on the sales record of Sparkle Light. In fact, the product has far exceeded our sales projections."

"That's wonderful," Desiree replied quickly. "I apologize if I gave out any information that was incorrect or misleading. Our news comes straight from UPI in New York, and we can't verify every—"

"Your commentary doesn't come from New York."

Her stomach tightened into a knot. Sam would kill her for this. Absolutely kill her. "True. Thanks so much for calling to straighten that out." She cued up the next song, struggling to keep her voice calm. "And now, we—"

"I'll take that trivia question now."

"What?"

"This is supposed to be a trivia contest, isn't it? Something about a free dinner for two?"

"Oh. Yes." Quickly, Desiree reached for a small box with the words THE TRIVIA GAME emblazoned across the lid. He really got a kick out of putting her on the spot, didn't he? Well, she'd give the jerk a hard one. Taking a deep breath to steady herself, she glanced through a few cards, then pulled one out. "Are you ready, Mr. Harrison?"

"Ready."

This'll get him, she thought. "What was the name of the first successful helicopter, and in what year was it built?"

Without a moment's hesitation, he said, "The FW-61. Germany built it in 1936."

Desiree's mouth dropped open. How did he know that? The damn obnoxious man had to be a trivia king on top of everything else. "That's correct! You're our winner for today." Trying to sound enthusiastic, she added, "Congratulations. If you'll stay on the line, I'll have someone explain where you can pick up your prize."

She punched the hold button on the phone. Play the next song, she instructed herself, going through the motions mechanically. And for God's sake, don't try to say anything cute. "Okay, coming up, three great tunes in a row from KICK 102 FM, your mellow music station."

Blowing out a relieved breath, Desiree punched another phone line and called the receptionist in the front office.

"Barbara? The contest winner's on line one. Would you

take care of him, please?" She hung up without waiting for a reply. The radio broadcast was piped throughout the building. She could count on Barbara to assess the situation.

Just then the studio door burst open. It was Sam.

"Since when did you become a stockbroker?" His eyes blazed in a deeply lined face surrounded by thinning grey hair. "No one asked for your advice about Sparkle Light. We play music around here, not the stock market."

"I know. I'm sorry. I just—"

"Stick to sports and the weather and leave Wall Street to the experts. Got it?" The door slammed.

Terrific, she thought.

The door opened again. "And another thing!" Sam yelled. "Don't chitchat with people on the air. We're a music station. If you want to do talk radio, get a job at KTLK."

She sighed deeply as the door slammed once more. She should never have commented on the news release. And she certainly shouldn't have talked so long on the air with Kyle Harrison.

Whatever had possessed her? She was lucky Sam hadn't fired her. One false move and a deejay was usually out the door. It's going to take a lot more than one rave newspaper review to keep me on the afternoon drive now, she thought with a frown.

Dejectedly, she studied the rotation chart taped to the window above the console. A hit tune—or type "A" song—was next. Reaching aside to the revolving music rack, she pulled the next cartridge in sequence from the row marked "A" and slipped it into the deck. It was a new

Anne Murray hit—a real heartbreaker, and one of her favorites.

Suddenly the lyrics of the song on the air caught her attention. The tone was tender, with an underlying melancholy.

Desiree's eyes crinkled with a familiar pang of sadness. She felt an affinity with the singer, as if the words about long and lonely nights were being sung solely to her, about her. She heaved a little sigh.

Her career demanded that she be self-sufficient and independent, and over the past five years she'd come to terms with that. In fact, she now preferred being on her own. So why was she partial to these tear-jerking love songs? Why did they always bring a lump to her throat?

She grabbed a pencil and scratch pad to jot down the titles of the songs coming up, so she could list them later on the air. But for some reason her pencil stood poised and motionless as a smooth, deeply masculine voice drifted into her consciousness. A voice that had sent a delectable shiver up her spine. A voice that a prince would be proud of. Too bad he'd turned out to be such a toad.

Several minutes later, a tall woman in a gaily striped sundress hurried into the studio, waving a chocolate candy bar.

"Sugar break. I know you like peanut butter cups, but the machine was out." Her black, curly hair was swept up into a messy bun, and her dark eyes were assessing. "Hey, what's the frown for? Did Sam read you the riot act?"

Desiree shrugged as she slid off her stool, grabbed the candy bar, and tore off its wrapper. "Yeah. But apparently, I'm still employed. For today, anyway."

She knew she shouldn't be eating this, but after what had just happened on the air, she needed something to cheer herself up. She took a bite of the chocolaty goodness and smiled with pleasure. "Mmmm. Hits the spot. Thanks, Barb. I've been eating celery all week. Another piece and I'd probably turn green."

Barbara pursed her lips in mock irritation. "As if you need to watch what you eat, you skinny thing."

"I do. Constantly. It's a cross all short people must bear. You Amazons don't know how lucky you are."

Barbara laughed and handed her a phone message. "Listen, I just got a call from a lady at Barney's, a new restaurant in Orange. They want to know if you'll host their opening-night party next month."

As she stared at the note, Desiree felt a stab of disappointment like a knife between the ribs. She couldn't do it, of course. It was impossible. "You gave her the usual polite refusal, I hope?"

Barbara shook her head. "No, I didn't. I told her you'd think about it."

"What's there to think about?" She handed back the note. "Just thank her and tell her I'm busy."

"You've got to stop hiding from your fans, Des. The lady raved about your voice. It'd be great publicity for you."

"Some great publicity. They're expecting Candice Bergen and instead they get Shirley Temple."

"Would you come off it? You might be short, but with your hair up, in the right kind of dress, you'd look glamorous as hell." She gestured emphatically with both hands. "And besides, you're gorgeous."

"I get what you're doing. But you can stop with the buttering up. My ego isn't that fragile."

"I'm not saying it to massage your ego. I'm saying it because it's true. I'd give a million bucks for a face like yours."

Desire shook her head, unconvinced. "Well, I'd give a million bucks to be six inches taller, like you, and wear your bra size."

Barbara laughed. "You're so dense. You don't know a good thing when you've got it. Plenty of men go gaga over petite women."

"I don't want men to go gaga over me. I'm perfectly happy the way I am."

"The hell you are. Only a nun would be happy living the way you do. When's the last time you went on a date? Two years ago? Three?"

"What's the point? You know what happened to my one attempt at marriage. Look at Dave. Look at Mike and John. Divorced, every one of them." Desiree finished the last bite of the candy bar and sighed. "Relationships and radio don't mix."

"Who's talking about relationships? I'm talking *date* here. A simple night out with a guy." Barbara shook her head in disgust. "Just because that husband of yours was a moron doesn't mean you should swear off men for the rest of your life. The other jocks sure haven't sworn off women."

Steve wasn't a moron, Desiree thought. But there was no sense arguing with Barbara about it. She glanced back at the digital countdown timer on the console. "I hate to eat and run, Barb, but I'm on in thirty seconds."

"Bye." Barbara backed up and paused in the doorway. "By the way, no matter what Sam said, I think you handled the guy on the phone like a pro."

"Thanks a bunch."

"No, I mean it. He pulled a dirty trick, calling on the contest line and springing all that stuff on you over the air. When he comes in to pick up his free dinner pass, I promise I'll be as obnoxious as possible."

Desiree grinned as Barbara pulled the door shut. "Do that."

FIVE-THIRTY. Desiree began to hum to herself. A half hour more and I'm out the door, she thought. She knew exactly what she was going to do when she got home: finish last night's Chinese take-out, take her phone off the hook, and curl up in bed with a glass of wine and a good book.

She waited for her cue, then said into the mike, "That was 'Songbird,' by Barbra Streisand. It's always been a special favorite of mine." Lowering her voice, she murmured throatily, "This is Desiree Germain. The summer equinox is next week, the longest day of the year. I hope you're taking advantage of the beautiful weather we're having, and all those extra hours of daylight. Why not take a walk on the beach this evening with your special someone? Tell them Desiree sent you. And don't forget to tell him ... or her ... that you love them."

She took off her headphones as the commercial break began. Three more tunes, she thought. Then the traffic report.

Behind her, she heard the studio door open and close quietly. Who was it now? she wondered. Before she could turn to look, a voice intoned:

"You do that well."

Desiree jumped up from her stool in surprise and whirled around, clutching her headphones.

A man stood a few feet away, studying her through twinkling dark-green eyes. "Sorry if I startled you. The red light was off."

"Who are you?" Desiree blurted, more annoyed than alarmed at this bold intrusion. But instinctively, she knew the answer. There was no mistaking the deep, resonant Radio Voice.

His next statement confirmed it.

"I'm Kyle Harrison."

CHAPTER 2

"I thought you were expecting me? Your receptionist said it was okay, as long as I was quiet."

Desiree stared at the man who had invaded her tiny studio, irritation prickling through her. *Barbara, you traitor.*

Another thought quickly followed.

This was Kyle Harrison?

Where was the sixtyish business executive she'd envisioned, the man who was built like Santa Claus?

This man looked to be in his early thirties. Incredibly young to be the sole owner of a multimillion-dollar corporation like Harrison Industries.

Conservatively cut, dark brown hair framed a face that was boyishly charming and at the same time disarmingly handsome. He wasn't overly tall, maybe five-foot-ten. His broad chest tapered to a narrow waist and hips. Light grey dress slacks hugged lean, well-proportioned legs and the short sleeves of his white dress shirt exposed muscular forearms.

This survey took barely a second, at which point Desiree realized that he was taking the same measure of her. His eyes traveled the length of her figure, from her bare legs to her tight-fitting cutoffs and T-shirt.

Despite herself, she felt her cheeks grow warm under his scrutiny. She tried to speak, but her tongue had uncooperatively glued itself to the roof of her mouth.

"So, there really is a beautiful woman behind the beautiful voice." His lips twitched slightly.

Desiree frowned at him. *Beautiful?* Hardly. He's just being polite, she thought, to mask his disappointment on seeing the real me. If he said one word about the electric-blue silk dress and the silver spiked heels, she'd kill him.

But he didn't. "I was afraid," he went on, "that I was going to find an old man operating some sort of electronic synthesizer, like in *The Wizard of Oz*."

"Funny," she threw back at him, finding her voice at last. "I expected you to be an old man, too."

"Did you?"

She nodded. What was he after? To walk into her studio while she was on the air—how brazen could you get?

He grinned. "I guess great minds think alike. Thanks for letting me come back here. I wasn't sure if you would, after what I said on the air."

"I *didn't* let you come back here. It was clearly Barbara's idea."

"Oh?" He paused, apologetic. "Sorry. I thought ... Well, anyway." He leaned one elbow on the high counter running the length of the small room and gave her another charming smile. "Your receptionist told me your boss had a coronary after my call and threatened to transfer you to

Siberia. I wanted to apologize in person for getting you in trouble."

Desiree felt her annoyance dissipate a tad. She fought to remind herself that she was angry with this man. *He embarrassed me on the air and caused my employer to scream at me. I will not let him charm me. I will not smile.*

"But I understand there are a few radio stations in Siberia, so you should be all right. If they're enlightened enough to hire female deejays in Russia."

Against her will, a small laugh bubbled up from inside her chest. She curbed it, shot him a wary glance. "I'm afraid I'd be out of luck in that market. I don't speak Russian."

"You never know. There are lots of English speakers in Russia. Maybe you could convince them to start an English language radio station."

"May be." She studied him for a moment. When he smiled, his eyes twinkled and lit up his entire face. It was a nice smile. Her gaze was drawn lower, to the riot of curly brown hair peeking out above the open neck of his shirt. A tie should be there, she thought. A monogrammed silk tie. A tingle raced through her.

Good grief. Why was she looking at his neck??

"When do you have to go back on the air?" he asked suddenly.

She whirled back to the console with a rush of panic. To her horror, the commercial break was nearly over. Another three seconds and she'd have had dead air. She was in enough trouble already without *that*. Quickly, she turned up the volume in the studio and made a smooth transition into the next tune.

She breathed out a sigh of relief. "That was a close call."

Lowering the volume again, she pulled out two cartridges from the music rack, feeling extremely self-conscious as she set up the next songs.

What was this man doing, standing in her booth and talking to her? It was totally against the rules! What had Barbara been thinking?

"I'm sorry if I'm distracting you." He still leaned against the counter, gazing at her with a compelling warmth. "I suppose I shouldn't be in here."

"No, you shouldn't." Of course, he was distracting her. She ought to tell him to get out. Now! Instead, she heard herself say: "But I don't have to talk for a while."

"That's too bad." His voice was deep and soft. "I like listening."

As his eyes locked with hers, a strange, inexplicable heat coursed through her body and she backed up into the stool, almost knocking it over. *What* was happening to her? She'd never reacted so strongly to any man before, not even when she first met Steve.

Apparently misinterpreting the cause of her confusion, he said with sudden concern, "Hey, if you're worried about your job, don't be. I just spoke with your manager and I think you're off the hook."

"What do you mean?"

"I just bought a sizable advertising package for Sparkle Light. It blankets the next three weeks and continues well into next year. I gave strict instructions that our spots run only during your show."

She stared at him, astonished. "That ought to make Sam dance in the aisles." And it certainly wouldn't hurt her standing there, either. She cocked her head, eyeing him curiously. "Why did you do that?"

"It seemed the least I could do, after getting you in so much hot water. I know I shouldn't have called when you were on the air. But it hit me wrong when you read that news release, and I—" He shrugged, running a hand through his hair. "Sometimes I do impulsive things."

Well, that makes one of us, Desiree thought. She rarely acted on impulse, preferred to think things through. Still … how could she possibly be angry with him now? Even though his presence in here was having the strangest effect on her ability to breathe.

He glanced around the small control room with obvious interest, appraising the equipment. "I haven't been in a radio station in years. This is fascinating. All right if I stay for a while and watch?"

"No!" She vigorously shook her head and was about to elaborate, when he raised one large palm as if stopping traffic.

"Okay. I understand. But before you kick me out, let me ask one favor." He reached into his shirt pocket and pulled out a white card. "I just happen to have a pass for a free dinner for two at—"

"Maximilian's," she finished for him with a laugh.

"Will you have dinner with me tonight?"

"What? No … sorry, I can't." Long years of refusing invitations conditioned her response. The words escaped before Desiree could stop them.

"Why not?"

"Because I …." she began, then hesitated.

He's a rich entrepreneur from Seattle, she cautioned

herself. You're a deejay from Anaheim. He's only asking you out because you're convenient, and he has a free dinner and no one to share it with.

"I ...." She'd always been the master of the instant, fabricated excuse. Why couldn't she think of anything? "I already have plans," she finished lamely.

"Oh." He nodded slowly, gazing at her. "I guess I shouldn't have expected you to be available on the spur of the moment. But I had to give it a try."

Inexplicably, a wave of disappointment welled up in Desiree's stomach. Was he going to give up so easily?

"Still, maybe we can work something out. These plans of yours. Tell me about them."

Don't you have eyes? a small voice taunted in the back of her mind. The man's an eleven on a scale of ten. What are you thinking? Go out with him!

"I promise you I'm harmless." He flashed her a boyish grin, raising his right hand in the traditional Boy Scout salute. "Trustworthy, loyal, helpful, friendly, courteous, cheerful ...."

"And obedient?" she interjected, recalling the oath her brother had enjoyed practicing with her in their youth.

"Scout's honor."

She couldn't stop her laugh. His smile radiated warmth and friendliness. You'll like me, it said. I already like you. She paused a moment, admiring his high sculpted cheekbones and the gracefully angled bridge of his nose. He was a handsome man, and he seemed to have a personality to match.

"Is it anything of critical importance?" he persisted. "Or could you get out of it?"

She considered. She hated to play right into Barbara's hands, but maybe her friend was right. Maybe she ought to enjoy some male company for a change. Since he lived over a thousand miles away, it would be all on her own terms. Dinner only, no danger of involvement, and no strings attached.

She looked him straight in the eye. "I was going to fly to England to have tea with the queen, but I suppose I could call and cancel."

"Tea at Buckingham Palace? Is that all? And here I was afraid it was something really special."

She shrugged. "That kind of invitation *is* rather run-of-the-mill. And let's keep our priorities straight. How often do I have the opportunity to dine with a soda-pop king?"

KYLE WAITED for her in the lobby until her shift ended at six o'clock. Fortunately, she found Barbara had gone for the day. Questions would certainly come tomorrow, but for now she was spared the embarrassment of a confrontation.

Since Desiree needed to change her clothes before dinner, Kyle followed in his car while she drove to the small ranch-style house she rented in Garden Grove.

His rental car was a sporty, dark-green Maserati. A car so flashy and expensive, it made her feel a little self-conscious about her used Toyota Camry. But, she reminded herself as she parked in the garage, she wasn't exactly a Maserati kind of girl. She lived on a budget and had to be practical in all her life choices, not just about cars.

Which made her question, again, the practicality of this last-minute dinner date. Was it sensible? Was it wise? Probably not, for about a dozen reasons. But she was committed. There was no going back now.

As Kyle stood behind her on the front steps of the house, it occurred to Desiree that she hadn't been expecting company. And Kyle clearly expected to come inside.

She unlocked the door, pushed it open a crack, and peered through the small opening into her living room, unsure in what condition she'd left the place. Cheeks flaming, she whirled around, yanking the door shut behind her. Her body collided with Kyle's in a sudden sharp impact, knocking the breath from her.

"Oh! Sorry!" Kyle grabbed her by the shoulders, not retreating an inch.

"You can't go in there," she gasped, pinned between him and the door.

"Why not?"

"It's a battlefield."

"I'm sure I've seen worse."

He stood so close she felt the warmth emanating from his body, and felt his breath, warm and sweet, on her cheek. She pressed her back against the door, tilted her head slightly, and looked up at him. "Trust me, you don't want to see it. Several people died there this morning, and the bodies haven't been cleared away yet."

He laughed. "Don't worry about it." His eyes slowly roved over her face, lingering for a long moment at her lips as if they were a mouth-watering dessert just out of his reach. His voice was somewhat rough when he spoke again. "I don't care, really. I didn't exactly give you much warning."

Her shoulders, under the pressure of his fingers, began to tingle, sending magnificent shooting sparks throughout her body. She was aware for the first time of the faint scent of a very pleasant masculine cologne.

She closed her eyes, enjoying the feel of his hands, the sense of his nearness. If only her living room wasn't such a mess, then he could come inside. She'd like to have him in her house. In her living room. In her—

No, Desiree! she cautioned. He's gorgeous and witty and incredibly sexy, but for God's sake, don't get carried away.

Tomorrow he'll fly back to his work and his life in Seattle, and you'll be back to your comfortable, uncomplicated … boring … lonely … routine.

She took a deep breath. "The thing is, there's … the dog."

He relaxed his grip on her shoulders and stepped back. "The dog?"

"A … vicious Doberman," she improvised. "Trained to attack strange men on sight."

He studied her for a moment with narrowed eyes, clearly aware that she was vamping. "Would it really embarrass you that much if I saw the way you keep house?"

"It really would."

"Why?"

"Because …." She hesitated, her shoulders still tingling from the remembered pressure of his fingers. "I don't want you to think—"

"Think what?"

She sighed in resignation. "That I'm a slob."

"I won't think that. I won't pass judgment, I promise."

"Okay. But remember: I warned you."

Gritting her teeth, her stomach quietly tying itself in knots, Desiree turned the knob, pushed the door open, and stepped inside.

She could have died. She wished she wasn't so disorderly. She preferred tabletops and counters to be clear and things to be organized and put in their places—really, she did. She just couldn't seem to get herself to do it on a regular basis.

Various items of discarded clothing lay draped across the back of the flowered chintz sofa. A wingback chair in a French blue-and-apricot print held a basket of clean laundry waiting to be folded. To her mortification a pair of panties and a lacy bra peeked out noticeably from the top of the pile.

Numerous pairs of shoes and sandals lay under the antique mahogany coffee table and at either side of the couch and chair. Magazines and books lay scattered on every surface, and partially filled water glasses on cork coasters seemed to be everywhere—on the ornate carved credenza, on the end tables, even on the mantel over the brick fireplace.

When would she grow out of that habit of taking a glass of water with her everywhere she went? When would she learn to stop taking off her shoes and socks and sweaters and leaving them wherever she happened to be sitting?

What was this man going to think of her?

Kyle took a step inside and paused, his lips set in a

noncommittal line. But the expression in his green eyes as they swept the cluttered room could only be called mild dismay. When she saw his gaze drift to the kitchen, where she'd stacked last night's dinner dishes on the counter, the color rose in her cheeks.

"I'll bet you're a neat freak. One of those folds-his-underwear-in-the-drawer types."

He nodded silently.

"I was afraid of that." She wanted to disappear into thin air, to start the day over again. Why had she ever agreed to this dinner date? It was madness! She scooped the clothes off the sofa and crumpled them into a tight ball against her thudding chest.

Any kind of relationship, even a short-term one, wasn't supposed to begin this way. A man, on seeing a woman's home for the first time, was supposed to be overwhelmed by its charm, and impressed by her impeccable taste in furniture and decor. Well, she'd certainly impressed him ... he was speechless!

"I told you it'd be a disaster. I'm sorry. All I can say in my own defense is ... it's not always this bad."

His smiled returned and he glanced at her with contrition. "Please, don't apologize or feel embarrassed. It's my fault. This has all been very impromptu. You weren't expecting visitors, and I shouldn't have been so pushy. But ... truth be told, this makes me feel right at home."

"Really?"

"Growing up, our house looked exactly like this. I have five sisters."

"Five sisters?" The notion made *her* smile. "How did you ever survive?"

"Being the only son, I got royal treatment. My own room. Special outings with my dad. It was great."

Desiree was grateful for his easygoing manner and apparently intentional effort to change the subject. "I just have one brother. Growing up in a big family must have been a lot of fun."

"It *was* fun." He sat down on the edge of the couch and absently arranged the scattered magazines and books into neat stacks. "I enjoyed playing Big Brother to a house full of beautiful women. My sisters are terrific. All of them, especially the twins."

"Twins! How wonderful. I used to dream I'd have twins of my own someday." Unintentionally, her eyes swept to his chest. Firm pectoral muscles rippled in sharp relief beneath his white summer dress shirt. Despite herself, she found herself imagining what that chest might look like without a shirt to cover it.

"Maybe you will." His voice brought her eyes up to meet his with a guilty start. Maybe she would what?

She stepped over to the credenza and turned on her stereo, letting the soft music of KICK-FM fill the room. "I hope you like mellow music."

"If I don't, I'm taking out the wrong girl."

"You have a point."

He studied the carved legs of the coffee table appreciatively. "Your furniture is beautiful. Is this an antique?"

"Yes. It belonged to my great-grandmother. All of this did. Do you like antiques?"

"I usually go for the more modern stuff, but I admire the craftsmanship on these old pieces. Especially the hand carving."

"If you like carving, you should see the detail work on the headboard of my four-poster bed. It's—" She broke off, blushing. Why did she say that? It almost sounded like an invitation.

"I'd love to see it."

"No!" She realized she had shouted the word and softened her voice. "The bedroom's even more of a disaster than the living room." She took several steps backward. "I'll go and change. Oh, can I get you something to drink?"

"No, thanks." He indicated two half-filled water glasses on the coffee table. "I'll just help myself to some of this if I get thirsty."

She choked back an embarrassed laugh. "I'll be back in five minutes." Turning, she fled down the hall. If she survived this evening with her sanity intact, it'd be a miracle.

I'M ONLY GOING out with this man once, Desiree told herself, as she fastened the tiny buttons up the front of her lavender cotton sundress. So, I might as well do it right.

What was it Barbara had said? In the right dress ... with your hair up ... you'd be as glamorous as hell. Well, the dress was far from glamorous, but it was the best she could do.

The flared skirt, trimmed at the hem by a long ruffle with matching crocheted lace, made her feel dainty and feminine, and the form-fitting bodice accentuated her tiny waistline. The deep orchid color contrasted with her fair complexion and seemed to bring a healthy glow to her face.

She pulled on high-heeled white sandals and picked up her brush, running it fiercely through the curls that cascaded down her back. She never wore her hair up. How would it look? She threw her head forward, grabbed the thick mass of hair and twisted it into a bun on top of her head.

Holding the bulky knot in place with one hand, she pulled a few wispy tendrils down around her forehead and ears. Standing up, she surveyed the effect in the beveled mirror above her dresser.

She looked ridiculous. Like a midget balancing a ball on her head.

Sighing, she shook her head vigorously, letting her hair fall into place in its natural side part. On a sudden impulse, she pulled out a delicate gold pendant from her jewelry box and fastened it around her neck.

When she returned to the living room, she found Kyle thumbing through a magazine, one arm draped across the back of the sofa, his legs stretched out in front of him. He'd buttoned his shirt and had put on a grey-and-blue-striped tie, which he must have brought in from his car. The last beams of fading sunlight streaming in through the front window burnished the gleaming copper highlights in his dark brown hair.

He looked totally natural and completely at ease, as if he made a daily habit of waiting in strange women's living rooms while they dressed for dinner. As she wondered if that were true, she thought he looked right somehow, relaxing there on her couch, as if he belonged there.

She smiled. "Glad to see you made yourself at home."

He tossed the magazine aside and looked up at her, his eyebrows lifting in admiration as he let out a low whistle. "Wow! You look terrific. I like your dress."

"This dress?" She felt her cheeks glow with pleasure but couldn't quite bring herself to meet his gaze. Fingering a corner of the long, ruffled hem, she said, "It's just an old thing. I'm sorry I don't have anything more chic, but—"

"You mean something in electric-blue silk, cut just off the shoulder?"

The color in her cheeks deepened. "Something like that."

"I prefer what you're wearing." He sprang up off the sofa with an athletic grace and covered the distance between them in a few quick strides. Tilting his head to one side, he regarded her the way an artist might study a painting. "That's a beautiful pendant."

"Thank you." She fingered the golden charm at her throat. Her favorite piece of jewelry, it depicted a tiny robin perched on a branch, singing its heart out. A small diamond twinkled in its eye.

"A songbird," he said. "Just like you."

His admiring gaze sent warmth spiraling through her and she couldn't help but smile. "It's over a hundred years old."

"Your great-grandmother's?"

She nodded. "I was named after her and was lucky enough to get some of her prized possessions."

"Well, she had excellent taste in furniture and jewelry. And in great-granddaughters."

He lifted one hand to the slope of her neck, sifted his

fingers through her hair, and held it up to the light, watching as the honey-brown strands fell softly back around her shoulders. He stared down at her for a long moment, his hand poised in midair, fingers tense and contracting.

Adrenaline pumped through Desiree's body as her eyes locked with his. What was going on in his mind?

A shiver tiptoed up her spine and her pulse quickened, as if anticipating a plunge into deep, icy waters. She blinked and lowered her eyes to his full, beautifully shaped lips. For some reason her thoughts scattered like petals in the wind and she struggled to reorganize them.

He lowered his hand and took a step back. She sighed with relief. Or was it regret?

"What do you say we go eat?" he said. "I'm starving."

CHAPTER 3

They sat at a window table, overlooking the wide expanse of white beach and rolling surf one flight of stairs below. Desiree had never been inside Maximilian's, although she'd often admired its stunning blend of plate glass and California redwood when she passed by during an evening walk on the Huntington Beach pier.

The interior was both comfortable and sophisticated with its nautical theme, tables draped in royal-blue, solid oak chairs, and vases of chrysanthemums scattered about.

She'd noticed several women's heads turn as she and Kyle made their way through the crowded restaurant to their table. No wonder. Kyle was easily the best-looking man in the room.

Their conversation flowed as smooth as the wine. The waiter, when he stopped to take their order, apologized for intruding, which made them laugh. Kyle seemed to want to know everything about her, and she was equally fascinated by him, each new detail of his life only whetting her appetite to learn more.

"How long have you been working at KICK?" Kyle asked after the waiter had served bowls of thick clam chowder.

"Two years."

"I read a review of your show in the *Times* on the flight down this morning. You're quite a celebrity."

"Not really." She shrugged. "It's a pretty small station. Few people recognize me by voice, and nobody knows me by sight. Thank goodness."

"What do you mean, thank goodness?" Kyle sipped his wine. "I thought all performers liked to be recognized."

"Not me. My voice ... I'm sure you've noticed. It's so ... throaty and low. It doesn't match up with the rest of me. People have kidded me about it since I was twelve. My listeners seem to expect some tall, curvaceous beauty. You can imagine how disappointed they are when they meet me."

"I wasn't disappointed," he said softly.

She felt a flutter in her stomach and wanted to look away but couldn't bring herself to break their eye contact. "You weren't?"

He shook his head. "I think your voice fits you perfectly." He seemed to want to say more.

She held her breath, waiting, wondering again what he was thinking. How would she respond if he told her, again, that she was beautiful? Would she believe it this time?

He glanced away. She swallowed her disappointment.

"While you were getting dressed, I took a look at your

library." He picked up his knife and spread sweet butter on a chunk of crusty sourdough bread. "Very impressive."

"My library?" She let go a short laugh. "You mean the books piled on the coffee table, or the ones stacked three-deep on the shelves?"

"Both. I saw quite a few of my favorite contemporary authors and titles. And you have all the classics that I love and re-read all the time: Shakespeare, Austen, Dumas, Dickens, Twain."

She smiled with delight as she took a spoonful of chowder. "I ran out of shelf space long ago, but books are like best friends. I can't stand to part with any of them."

"Me neither. My whole living room's lined with bookshelves. Reading's the best kind of company for someone living on their own."

"I know what you mean. Reading keeps me from noticing how lonely I am. I read while I eat, before I go to sleep—"

"It does get lonely, doesn't it?"

She froze, her spoon halfway to her mouth. His eyes locked with hers across the table.

"Do you like living alone?" he asked softly.

A current of awareness seemed to travel across the space between them. She lowered her eyes, toyed with the blue linen napkin in her lap. "I don't mind it. I've been alone for five years. I guess I'm used to it by now." She laughed lightly. "I'd better be used to it, anyway. I tried marriage once. It didn't even last a year. I'll never try it again."

"Never say *never*. Maybe you just married the wrong man."

"I don't think so. The divorce was inevitable, no matter who I'd married." She hoped he wouldn't pursue the subject further. She considered the last months before the divorce to be the lowest point in her life. She preferred to forget them.

"How about you?" she asked. "Have you ever been married?"

"No."

"Really? Thirty years old and never been hitched?"

A smile tugged at the corners of his lips. "Thirty-four."

She expected him to add more, to explain that he, too, was against the idea of marriage. After all, she reasoned, a man this handsome, this charming and successful, could hardly have escaped marriage unless he had an aversion to the institution in general. But he said nothing for several heartbeats, just continued to look at her over the rim of his wineglass.

She felt her skin grow hot under his gaze and she glanced out the window beside them, where the setting sun painted a watercolor wash of purple, pink, and gold across the sky. A few hardy surfers still sat astride their boards, rising and falling on the water's dark surface like bobbing ducks.

"I guess *we* can't get married, anyway," he remarked casually.

Her eyes flew up to meet his, astonished by the stab of disappointment those words had brought.

"We'd have two copies of every book in the house," he teased.

She laughed. "True. It'd be so ... redundant. And since I

can't throw anything away, it'd create quite a storage problem."

He grinned in response but didn't comment. She had no idea what to say next. To her relief, the waiter chose that moment to arrive with their dinners.

For Desiree: a platter of mesquite-broiled halibut, with wild rice, French-cut green beans, and honeyed carrots on the side. When the waiter placed Kyle's meal before him, she felt a pang of envy rise in her chest.

He'd ordered lobster. Fresh American lobster, flown in that morning from Maine.

"Ahh. Look at this beauty." Kyle spread his cloth napkin across his lap. The lobster reclined on a bed of rice in reddish-orange splendor, head and tail intact, arched shell up. The detached claws, already cracked, were arranged beside a cup of melted butter. She could smell its rich scent across the table.

She watched him pierce a wedge of lemon with his fork and squeeze it into the butter. Her mouth watered. He used the fork to scoop a large piece of white meat from one claw, dipped it into the lemon butter and lifted it to his lips. He caught her eye and stopped, his fork poised in midair.

"I *told* you to order the lobster," he said.

It was true. The waiter had also highly recommended it.

But the complimentary dinner pass stated that lobster was not included. Favorite food or no, they had come for a free dinner, and she'd insisted that at least one of them should take advantage of it. Besides, she could eat for half a week for the same price.

"This is fine." She quickly tasted a piece of halibut.

Firm. Meaty. Mild. One hundred and twenty-five calories per four ounce serving. The healthier choice. "Delicious," she lied.

"Try this." Kyle extended his forkful of lobster across the table.

"Your first bite? No, I couldn't—" Before she could protest further, he popped the morsel into her mouth. She closed her eyes and chewed, savoring the moist, buttery flavor. "Oh, yum. What a treat. It's been ages."

She heard his laugh, followed by a scraping sound. When she blinked open her eyes, the lobster stared back at her. Her own plate sat in front of Kyle.

"I got a sudden, uncontrollable craving for halibut." He picked up the plastic bib the waiter had brought and handed it to her across the table. "This will look better on you than it would on me, anyway."

Her eyes widened. "No, Kyle. I wouldn't dream of taking your dinner."

"Go ahead. Enjoy."

Hesitantly, she added, "Are you sure you don't mind?"

"I'm sure."

She tied the bib around her neck and pounced. Picking up the lobster's steaming shell in two hands, she turned it soft side up and arched it until the tailpiece pulled loose from the body. With one deft movement she bent back the tail flipper section until it cracked off. Lifting the tailpiece downside up, she expertly inserted the lobster fork through the hole left by the flippers and pushed the tail meat out through the open end.

"I can see," he said, watching her, "just how rarely you get lobster."

"It's only been rare recently." She took a bite, pausing for a moment of appreciative silence as she chewed and swallowed. "I lived in Maine for a year and a half. Every chance I got, I'd buy a lobster or two at the wharf. Three dollars a pound, plucked right out of the tank, and cooked while you wait."

His eyes never left her face. "No wonder you can't stand the prices here."

She broke off one of the lobster's legs and softly closed her mouth around the open end. With lips and tongue she slowly and gently sucked out the contents. Across from her and watching, Kyle drew a single breath that was out of rhythm with the others. His green eyes glittered with sudden brightness, and a smile lingered on his mouth.

All at once aware of what he might be thinking, Desiree felt her cheeks flush red and hot. She swallowed hard. Picking up one of the legs, she held it out to him. "Would you like to share?"

He shook his head. "Not just now." Finally, he picked up his knife and fork.

As they enjoyed the meal, they talked. Desiree found herself relaxing as the conversation moved from one topic to another. They discussed their favorite movies, discovered that they listened to similar music, and both enjoyed the theater.

She told him about the wonderful Victorian house in Pasadena where she had grown up, and how sad she'd been when her parents sold it and moved to Florida.

Kyle had lived in Seattle all of his life, he said. His parents and most of his relatives still lived there.

"Do you come to Southern California often?"

"Just a few times a year on business. Have you ever been to Washington state?"

"No."

"It's beautiful. Everything's green all year round. From my office window on the tenth floor, I've got a fantastic view of downtown Seattle and Elliot Bay."

"That sounds wonderful. Is it true what I've heard, though? That it rains nine months out of the year in Seattle?"

"Yes," he admitted, "but you get used to it. And when the sun shines, the sky is the bluest blue you've ever seen."

"We have blue skies too," she said defensively.

He laughed. "I've seen days where it comes close." He folded his napkin on the table and sat back in his chair. "Your weather *is* enviable, no doubt about it. But it's a little too hot for me."

"Not always. Today you could have fried pancakes on the sidewalk, but it's generally mild."

"I like having four seasons."

"Well, after a few summers in Tucson and winters in Detroit and Bangor, Maine, I'll take this climate any day. I don't know how long my gig will last, but I'm grateful to be here, especially since I finally got my own drive time show. Seven years of nights is enough for anyone."

"Seven years? Why'd it take so long to get a decent shift?"

"There's a built-in prejudice in this business against women. We're stuck with the worst hours for the least pay. Midnight to dawn—they still call it the Women's Shift. And that's one of the nicer names for it." Five years ago, she explained, you rarely heard a woman on the air during the afternoon, even in Southern California. "They're a bit more progressive here. Most deejays would kill for the chance to work in L.A. or Orange County. It's the hottest market in the country."

"Why? Because you're so close to the television and film industries?"

"That's a big part of it. A jock with a good voice can earn good money on the side in commercials, voice-overs, and animation—or so I'm told, I haven't explored that yet. But the biggest attraction here is the pay scale." She finished her wine. With instinctive awareness Kyle reached for the bottle and raised an eyebrow in her direction. At her nod, he refilled her glass.

"AFTRA, our union, takes care of us," she went on, "sees to it that we have decent wages and working conditions. Other markets aren't so lucky. Just a few years back, I was working ridiculous hours for starvation wages."

"Really? I imagined deejays were paid handsomely. Like television stars."

"Far from it. This might be show biz, but we're on the bottom rung of the ladder."

She reached across the table to offer him her last bite of lobster. He smiled and leaned forward, then closed his lips around her fork. At the same time his hand closed around hers. A spark shot through her veins at the warmth of his touch.

"Nice," he said, his eyes lighting up appreciatively. She wasn't sure if he was referring to the taste of the food or the feel of her hand.

He took the fork from her and set it down, leaned his elbows on the table, and wrapped her hand in both of his.

"Why have you lived in so many places? Detroit, did you say? Tucson? And Maine?"

"Change of jobs." His hands, she noticed, were large and covered with dark springy hairs. They felt warm and dry and wonderful against hers. "In this business after a year at the same station you're practically considered an old-timer. Unemployment's always looking over your shoulder."

"Why is it so hard to keep a job?"

"Ratings."

The candlelight flickered across the side of his face and brought a reddish gleam to his day's growth of whiskers. She wondered if his cheeks felt smooth or rough to the touch. She wondered what color his beard would be. Dark brown, like his hair? Or more coppery, like its highlights?

"Ratings?" he asked.

She took a deep breath and continued. "If the station isn't doing well, the program director often wipes the slate clean and starts off with all new talent. Or he might decide to switch the format of the station from music to Talk Radio or All News, which also requires a whole new crop of people. And there are so many young kids, beating down the door to take our jobs. If we forget to play one spot or say one thing the P.D. doesn't like, he might decide to fire us, try somebody else."

"Sounds too precarious for my blood."

"Not me. Once you're in the business, it's like a compulsion. Any other job would pale in comparison."

She watched, transfixed, as his fingers gently rubbed across the back of her knuckles. The tingling sensations that began there raced the length of her arm, down through her body. She wondered what it would feel like if his fingers were to touch her in more intimate places, in places that had been so long denied ….

She tore her eyes away and looked down at the table, drawing a mental curtain over the pictures forming in her mind. To her surprise, their plates were gone, replaced by steaming cups of coffee. When had the busboy stopped by?

"Cream?" he asked, letting go of her hand.

"Y … yes," she managed in a strangled voice. *Stop thinking of him that way,* she scolded herself. *You'll drive yourself crazy.*

She took the pitcher of cream from him and allowed herself a small dab. "We've talked far too much about me. Tell me, how'd you come to be such a powerhouse in the business world?"

He answered her questions simply, but with enthusiasm. He seemed proud of his achievements but showed no trace of conceit or arrogance. He studied both business and engineering in college, he told her, worked for a while at Boeing, and eventually decided to start his own company to manufacture tooling and parts for aircraft. The business mushroomed after a few years, and he invested in other companies, including an engineering firm. Sparkle Light was his latest acquisition.

"Why a soft drink company?" she asked, after a rather bemused busboy had refilled their coffee cups for the third time. "Everything else is related to aerospace. It doesn't seem to fit in."

He shrugged. "It looked profitable. Keeps things interesting."

Kyle paid the bill but gave no indication that he wanted to leave. Desiree was in no hurry to go, either.

"And you started the whole thing on a shoestring." She shook her head in amazement. "I'll bet when the other kids were riding bikes or playing cowboys, you were out learning how to close business deals."

He didn't answer right away. Instead, he gazed out the window at the midnight-blue sky, which descended toward the rippling dark water in gradually lighter shades of blue.

"As a kid, I never gave business a thought," he said in a low voice. "From the time I saw Cary Grant in *Only Angels Have Wings,* all I ever wanted to do was fly. I was crazy about airplanes, helicopters, spaceships—anything that flew. I made models, read every book I could find on the subject. I vowed I'd someday be a commercial pilot or join the air force."

"So that's how you knew the answer to that obscure trivia question about the helicopter. I thought for sure I had you stumped on that one."

He grinned and reached for her hand again across the table. "Lucky for me I got it right."

Why did she feel such a sizzling jolt each time he touched her hand? "Then why didn't you become a pilot? What happened to change your mind?"

"I didn't change my mind." To her surprise and disappointment he jerked his hand away. "Circumstances prevented me from becoming a pilot. I thought designing airplanes would be a good substitute for flying them, but …." He remained silent, staring moodily into his empty coffee cup.

43

She read resentment and suppressed frustration in his gaze. Her fingers ached to reach out and touch his cheek, to smooth away the lines of tension she saw there. As she debated the advisability of such a move, he abruptly pushed back his chair and stood up.

"Well, what do you say we go, before they start charging us rent for this table?"

Desiree fumbled for her purse and quickly followed Kyle out of the restaurant. Conversation was strained during the twenty-minute drive back to her house.

She sank back into the Maserati's deep leather-cushioned seat and watched the darkened rows of stucco housing tracts whiz by. What had prevented Kyle from becoming a pilot? she wondered. He'd been so free to tell her everything else about himself. Why did he suddenly become withdrawn when that subject was brought up?

He pulled into her driveway, got out, and walked her to her front step.

She considered asking him in, then thought better of it. She reached into her purse and rummaged for her key. "Well, good night, Kyle. Thank you for—"

"Wait." He placed one hand lightly on her arm. "There's something I want to say. Do you know why I came to the station tonight?"

Her eyes lifted in surprise. "To pick up the free dinner pass." As soon as she said it, she realized how ridiculous it sounded. What did a man like Kyle need with a free dinner pass?

"I came to meet you."

"Oh," she said, flattered and flustered at the same time.

"When I heard you on the radio, I kept wondering what

you looked like. I couldn't stop thinking about you. I wanted to know if there was a living, breathing woman behind the sexy talk and the sexy voice."

His reference to her on-air role made her blush. "It's not really me, you know. It's just a part I play. I do it because my program director likes it. It keeps the ratings up."

"I think it's great. I'll bet every red-blooded male in Southern California is as curious as I was. You must get hundreds of calls every week. Bags of mail."

"I do get my share. All kinds of men write me letters and ask me out."

His voice lowered as he studied her. "Ever take anyone up on it?"

"Never."

He placed his hands on her waist. "Never?"

She shook her head. He was standing so close. Her body began to tremble from the sudden erratic beating of her heart. The heat from his hands was a sizzling presence at her sides. She wanted to wind her hands around his neck and pull him against her, until she could feel the warmth of his body against hers. "Never," she repeated.

"Well, I consider myself very lucky then," he said softly.

She swallowed hard. "I still can't believe Barbara sent you back to my studio today when I was on the air. Even if you did buy a year full of ads. It is *so* not allowed."

"I thought it was a bit unorthodox, but I couldn't pass up the opportunity. 'If Desiree finds out you're here,' she said, 'she'll refuse to see you and won't leave until ten o'clock. So, you'd better just barge in.' I hope you didn't mind."

"I didn't."

His hand slipped from her waist to the small of her back and drew her closer. A tremor ran through her as her softness molded against the hard contours of his thighs and chest.

He lifted his other hand and gently grazed his fingertips up the soft whiteness of her neck to rest briefly on her earlobe. He held her gaze for a moment, his eyes smoldering in the reflected glow of a nearby streetlamp.

"You have beautiful eyes," he murmured.

Her breath caught in her throat. "No, I don't."

"You do. I've never seen eyes that color. They remind me of molten gold."

"Molten gold?"

He nodded. "Rare. And beautiful. Like you."

Desiree's heart pounded in her ears. No one had ever said that to her before. His words washed over her, and for a moment, she allowed herself to feel rare ... and beautiful.

But just for a moment.

She knew he wanted to kiss her. And she knew now that she wanted his kiss, hungered for it. But she shouldn't let it happen. The magnetic pull she felt toward him was overpowering. The very touch of his hand had caused fire to rush through her veins, threatening to consume her with need. Once she felt his mouth on hers, she knew she'd be lost.

He was only here for a day or two. There was no telling if he'd ever be back. And she couldn't get involved with Kyle, with any man, even if he lived next door.

How long would she be at KICK? Another year if she was lucky? Then, as always, she'd have to move on. She could never stay in one city long enough to make any relationship last.

Kyle Harrison already lived more than a thousand miles away. No matter how strong her attraction was to him, she knew that long-distance relationships didn't work. She'd been down that road before with Steve, and her heart still hadn't quite mended. It would be emotional suicide to try it again.

"It's getting late." She tried to pull free of his embrace, but his arms tightened around her.

"Is it?"

"I have to be at the station early tomorrow. And you must have a long drive back to your hotel."

His body moved against her as he shrugged. "That depends on where I stay."

"What do you mean?" She wrenched herself out of his arms and stepped back in sudden alarm. Did he think she'd let him stay here?

"I had reservations at a hotel in L.A. and was on my way there from my meeting when I heard you on the radio. I got kind of sidetracked."

"Oh. I'm sure the hotel held your reservation," she said quickly. "You can call them to see. And if not, there must be plenty of other—"

"Relax." His eyes narrowed as he watched her. "I'll find a room somewhere. Don't worry about it. I'll be fine."

She let out a relieved breath. "How long did you say you're here for?"

"I go back tomorrow afternoon. Can I call you sometime? After I get back to Seattle?"

"Sure," she said, knowing he wouldn't.

"Good."

She climbed the step and unlocked the front door, her heart still pumping erratically. This is what she wanted, wasn't it? A quick and final goodbye?

She turned back to face him, one hand on the doorknob. "Thank you for dinner."

"Nothing to thank me for. Your dinner was free." He smiled.

"The lobster was a real treat."

"I'm glad you enjoyed it. Thanks for going out with me. It's been a wonderful evening."

"Yes. It has." She wanted to tell him how much she'd enjoyed his company, that she'd like to see him again, even though she knew it would never happen and would be hopeless even if it did. All she said was: "Good night."

"Good night," he replied.

Goodbye, she amended silently.

He turned and was gone.

CHAPTER 4

Desiree slept badly. What little sleep she did manage to catch was filled with dreams of Kyle. She went for her morning jog and then fixed her usual breakfast—half a grapefruit, a poached egg, a cup of black coffee—but she couldn't seem to get him out of her mind.

One date, that's all it was, she reminded herself. That's the only reason you went. No danger of involvement. No strings attached.

Ha, she thought as she rinsed off yesterday's dishes and slid them into the dishwasher. So much for not getting involved. So much for no strings attached. From the moment they met she'd felt a wild attraction to the man, and she couldn't do a thing about it.

Activity, she told herself. That's what you need. Anything to get your mind off Kyle. All at once the clutter in her house seemed a welcome challenge. She spent the better part of the morning clearing away the scattered books and clothes in the living room, vacuuming and dusting, and scrubbing the kitchen floor. The bedroom was still a mess, but it would have to wait. Shortly before noon, pleased with her accomplishments, she locked up and left for work.

She slipped through the side door at the station, hoping Barbara was too busy to notice her arrival. No such luck. Desiree had just begun taping a routine for her Comedy Corner series when Barbara strode through the recording studio door.

"Des! There you are. I hope you've forgiven me for—" Barbara stopped short at the sight of Desiree's grim expression. "Oh no. You aren't mad at me, are you?"

"Yes, I'm mad at you. That was some trick you played, sending that guy back here yesterday."

"I didn't see any harm in it. He was such a charmer. And after he'd spent all that money on an advertising package, I couldn't say no."

"Oh yes you could have."

"Are you going to tell me what happened? Did you go out with him?"

"Yes."

Barbara gasped in delight. "And?"

"Leave me alone."

"No way! I have to know!"

"We went out to dinner," Desiree responded reluctantly. "Then he took me home."

"That's it?"

"That's it."

"Why? Didn't you like him?"

"Yes, I liked him.

"Then why ....?"

"Barbara, just back off, please?"

"Tell me you're going to see him again."

Desiree let out a long sigh. "How do you suggest I do that? He lives in Seattle."

"So what? That's what airplanes are for. Des, the man is *gorgeous*. I thought for sure you'd go for him. And he was so nice, the way he fixed things with Sam."

"He *is* nice. But I've told you, relationships and radio don't mix."

"They could, if you would—"

"I don't want to talk about it. Okay?"

Barbara's hands flew up in exasperation. "You're impossible." She turned to leave, nearly colliding with a stunning floral arrangement carried aloft in the doorway.

"For me?" Barbara said with a teasing smile.

"Sorry, sweetheart." Tom peered around the flowers and grinned at Desiree. "They're for this lovely lady. Better tell me where you want 'em pronto, 'cause this thing weighs a ton."

Desiree stared at the brilliant red buds. A dozen long-stemmed red roses were surrounded by ferns and baby's breath in a tall, cut-glass vase.

"Just set them on the counter, Tom. Thanks." She squeezed in front of Barbara and grabbed the small, attached envelope. Turning her back, she pulled out the card inside. It read simply:

To the loveliest woman with whom I've ever shared a lobster.
Kyle.

Her stomach seemed to trip over itself. She realized she'd been holding her breath and let it out in a long, deep sigh. Aware of Barbara's tall form peering over her shoulder, she clasped the card to her chest. "This is private, if you don't mind."

"Just went out to dinner, huh? Never going to see him again, huh?" Smirking with satisfaction, Barbara tossed her dark hair and slipped out the door.

DESIREE GLANCED up at the clock. It was 3:06 p.m. How could only two minutes have gone by since she last checked the time? The day usually zoomed by. Today, time crawled. The roses' perfume filled the small studio, doing nothing to decrease the feeling of light-headedness that had descended on her the moment they'd arrived.

She wondered what time Kyle's plane left for Seattle. Was he still in a meeting? Had he already gone? Would he call before he left?

She wanted to thank him for the flowers, but realized she'd never even asked for his home address or phone number. Should she call information or leave a message at his office?

It was impossible to concentrate. Memories of the way he had looked across the dinner table by candlelight, the intimate way he'd held her hand, the expression in his eyes when they'd stood on her front porch, played over and over in her mind like a movie on a continuous reel.

Several times she found herself singing along with the

music on the air. She'd forget to notice when a song began to fade and nearly miss her cue for the next tune. She forgot to keep track of what she played and couldn't think of a single witty thing to say.

The Trivia Game contest was completely lacking in excitement. She dutifully screened each call, her heart leaping with each punch of the button, hoping it might be Kyle. It wasn't.

Somehow, she managed to finish her shift. At six o'clock, she strolled nonchalantly into the reception area and asked if anyone had called or come by.

"Sorry," Barbara said as she packed up to leave. "His Gorgeousness has not appeared within these walls. Better luck tomorrow."

Disappointment curled inside her stomach like a tightly wound spring. He'd left without saying goodbye.

She retreated to the recording studio, began to dub comedy spots and humorous sound effects from albums onto tape. Between seven and eight o'clock someone dropped off a hamburger and fries, and she dug into them hungrily.

By nine-thirty her long day had caught up with her. Feeling tired and dejected, she returned the albums to the station's library, grabbed her purse and sweater, and headed for home.

She parked in her garage and was in the process of yanking down the garage door when she heard the approaching roar of a car. Tires squealed. A dark-green Maserati turned into her driveway and stopped before her, engine humming, headlights glaring.

Kyle leaned his head out the open car window. "Just getting home?"

Astonishment and excitement tingled through her at the same time. She couldn't believe how glad she was to see him. Glad? she asked herself. Understatement of the year. Try ecstatic.

She crossed to his car, fighting to hold back a smile. The smile won. "Broads in broadcasting are dedicated souls," she told him.

"No kidding. Remind me to believe you if you ever say you have to work late."

She leaned on the window frame. In the glow of the streetlamp she could see he wore a light tan suit, blue shirt, and matching striped tie. He looked gorgeous.

"Thanks for the roses. They're beautiful."

"My pleasure."

His hair was wind tousled. She ached to run her fingers through it. He must like to drive with the window open, she thought, to feel the wind on his face. So did she.

"Why aren't you in Seattle?"

"My meeting ran later than I expected. Much later, in fact. Looks like I'll be here for another day. I was with a potential client and he insisted on wining and dining me. I couldn't wait to get out of there. Finally, I told him I had a date for tonight and made my escape."

"Do you?" she asked.

"Do I what?"

"Have a date for tonight."

"That depends on your answer to my next question."

"Which is ....?"

"Do you like ice cream?"

She laughed. "Do ballerinas wear toe shoes?"

His lips widened in a devastating smile. "Well then, hop in."

Hop in? Should she? She studied his face in the moonlight and decided he was too handsome for her own good. She'd love to go out with him. What sane woman wouldn't? But if she spent another few hours in his presence, she'd only make it harder for herself when he left the next day.

She swept a lock of hair behind one ear and gestured toward the cutoffs and T-shirt she was wearing. "My outfit may be fine for my job, Mr. Harrison, but I doubt if it's appropriate for a night on the town."

His eyes traveled the length of her legs with an appreciative glow. "As a matter of fact, I'm the one who's overdressed for the place I have in mind. As I recall, the sign outside said Shoes and Shirt Required. It didn't say a thing about pants."

She laughed again. "I don't know, Kyle. I—"

"Come on, lady." He reached across the car and pushed open the passenger door. "Be daring. I promise you a good time."

Reason and caution deserted her. She circled the car and climbed in. "You're the last person I expected to find on my doorstep tonight," she said after he'd backed out and gunned the sports car through her quiet neighborhood onto Beach Boulevard.

He gazed at her briefly before turning back to the wheel. "I couldn't leave without seeing you again."

He asked about her day, probed with endless questions, and seemed to be fascinated by what she considered the most obscure details. He said he'd spent the day in boring meetings, and the high point of his day was dinner.

"You'll never guess what I ordered."

Their eyes met. "Lobster," they said in unison. Their laughter was immediate and infectious.

"I hope your client didn't steal it away from you."

"No. But it didn't taste the same without you there," he said, his voice low and deep.

She felt that now-familiar flutter in her stomach and had to turn her face to the window to hide her blush and the wash of sexual desire she knew must be written there.

He drove to Huntington Beach and parked just a few blocks down from the restaurant where they'd eaten the night before. "I saw this place last night." He indicated the small ice-cream parlor in front of them. "What do you say to a double cone and a walk on the beach?"

"Fantastic." Desiree jumped out of the car and pulled on her lightweight sweater. The air felt cool and pleasant, with the sound of nearby crashing waves and the pungent, salty smell of the sea.

Kyle pushed open the glass door of the ice-cream parlor and they stepped inside the dimly lit interior. A teenage girl in a white apron smiled at them as she vigorously rubbed the long glass counter with a rag. "You're just in time. I was shutting off the lights. I'm about to close up."

Kyle stepped up to the display case and raised an eyebrow at Desiree inquiringly. "What'll you have?"

She pondered for a moment over the vast array of different flavors, finally tapping the glass above a container of mint chocolate-chip. "I could go more exotic, but I think I'll stick to my favorite flavor tonight."

He glanced at the barrel of pale green ice cream below the glass. "Oh? Strawberry?"

She stared at him, her lips parted in surprise. Strawberry? Was he kidding? "Are you color blind?"

She blurted the question without thinking, presuming he was just joking. The look in his eyes told her it was no laughing matter. His face reddened slightly, and he averted his eyes, his mouth drawn into a tight line. "Why? What'd I say?"

"Nothing, it's just that ...." She could have kicked herself. Why hadn't she been more tactful? "This flavor. It's mint chip. It's green."

"Oh." He shrugged off his embarrassment. "Yes, I'm color blind." He turned quickly to the girl behind the counter, who was staring at them curiously. "She'll have two scoops. Mint chip. The green stuff." He ordered fresh peach, paid for the cones, and guided her outside.

"I'm sorry, Kyle," she began. "I didn't—"

"Forget it." His clipped tone warned her to drop the subject. But why? She was sorry she'd embarrassed him, but color blindness was no big deal. Why was he so touchy about it?

"Come on." He grabbed her by the hand, urging her to hurry.

His enthusiasm was contagious. She forgot everything in her sudden need to be closer to the lapping surf. They found a staircase at the end of the block and bounded down the concrete steps to the beach.

They took off their shoes and left them on the bottom step. He rolled up his pant legs and she laughed, telling him he looked like a schoolboy in knickers. He threatened to capsize her ice-cream cone if she didn't behave herself.

They joined hands again and raced across the wide stretch of cool, gritty sand, which glowed pale grey in the moonlight. He slowed a few yards from the water's edge, and they strolled along in silence. She enjoyed the feel of the cold, wet, dark sand beneath her feet and the sweet, frosty taste of the ice cream.

"Isn't this nice?" He grinned, squeezing her hand and swinging their arms.

"Yes." A laugh bubbled up inside her chest. "I haven't done anything this spontaneous—or fun—in ages."

"Why not?"

"I don't know. I guess because I've worked nights for so long. My social life has been pretty nil."

"Work is important, but you have to make time for fun." He glanced at her. "You don't strike me as an overly serious type. And from what I've read, people who are ... that is to say, people who create clutter ...."

"Create clutter?" She punched him lightly on the arm. "How rude. Is it my fault if the maid decided to take the week off?"

"People who create clutter," he went on, his lips twitching with suppressed laughter, "are often marvelously relaxed. They don't need everything to be in order around them. They're imaginative, impulsive, open to new ideas. They respond to the moment. Is that true of you?"

"Sometimes."

A challenging look crept into his green eyes, and she sensed he intended more by the question than appeared on the surface.

"I just haven't been around many other crazy, spontaneous people lately," she added.

"It's time we changed that."

The shiver that ran through Desiree's body had nothing to do with the breeze that whipped her hair across her cheek. She pulled her sweater more tightly around her.

"Cold?" he asked.

"I'm fine."

"You can have my jacket if you'd like." He began to shrug out of the tailored suit jacket.

"No thank you, that's not necessary." She flashed him a grin. "Anyway, the sleeves would probably hang down to my knees."

"I'm not that tall. Only five-ten."

"You seem tall to me."

He finished the last bite of his ice-cream cone. "That's because you're such a tiny pixie yourself." When he saw her grimace at his choice of words, he stopped and slipped an arm around her waist. "Hey! What's wrong with being short?"

She almost forgot his question, she was so entranced by the feel of his body next to hers, and the sound of his voice against her ear.

"Being short is a pain. I can't reach the top shelves in my kitchen. I can't reach the dipstick to check the oil in my car. Clothes off the rack never fit me right. Every time I buy a pair of pants, I have to cut off at least four inches at the hem. And since I'm so small, it seems I've had to fight all my life to be noticed, to be respected."

"You didn't have to fight to catch *my* attention," he said softly. "I think you're the perfect height."

"Perfect?" To disguise her rising discomposure, she made a face and said in a teasing voice, "You think five-foot-two-and-five-eighths is perfect?"

Chuckling, he drew her closer. "Do you have any idea what a relief it is to be out with a woman who doesn't have to worry about whether or not she'll be too tall for me if she wears heels?"

She laughed, loving his ability to put her at ease. "That's one problem I've never had, no matter who I've gone out with. And thank goodness you're not any taller. I practically have to bend my neck in half to look up at you as it is."

"At last, a woman who can appreciate my height." He went silent for a moment, smiling, and then nodded toward her cone. "You know, except for the chocolate chips in your ice cream, the peach and mint chip look exactly the same color to me."

She searched his face, relieved at the lack of embarrassment she saw there, but unsure how to respond. The breeze had ruffled his hair and she stifled an impulse to brush the unruly strands off his forehead. "What do they look like to you?"

"Sort of a light beige, I guess. I assume they're completely different colors?"

She nodded. "Do you have trouble seeing all colors?"

"No. Mainly reds and greens. I don't know what purple looks like to you. To me it looks blue."

His nearness and the mild fragrance of his cologne were doing strange things to her heartbeat. She finished her cone, stepped back and knelt in the sand a few feet away and rinsed her hands in the gently flowing surf.

A sudden thought occurred to her. Last night, he said he'd wanted to be a pilot, but that circumstances had prevented it. With a jolt of painful awareness, she remembered reading somewhere that normal color perception was mandatory for air force and commercial pilots.

She stood up and shook her hands dry. Hesitantly she asked, "That's what kept you from becoming a pilot, isn't it? Being color blind?"

"Yes."

"Why is color perception so important?"

"Warning lights, mainly. In military and commercial aircraft, each light in the cockpit conveys a specific message. Green is status quo. Amber's a warning. Low oil pressure, that kind of thing. Red's an emergency situation. There are lights on the wing tips, too. At night the color tells you if other aircraft are approaching or heading away. And if your radio should malfunction, the tower can signal landing instructions in code with colored lights. They can't take a chance on someone who might misinterpret the signals." He let out an ironic laugh. "I passed all the other tests with flying colors—ha ha—but ...." He shrugged.

"If that's what you really wanted to be, I'm sorry."

"Don't be. I don't regret it, not anymore." He took her hand again and they continued on down the beach. "I've become successful at what I do, and it didn't keep me on the ground. I may not be able to fly for an airline or the air force, but I can still fly. I'm restricted to daytime flight, that's all."

"Really? You have a pilot's license?"

"I do. I'm licensed to fly both private planes and helicopters. I own a twin-engine Bonanza. I use it for pleasure outings, short trips. It's a great little machine." He gestured animatedly with one hand. "There's a special kind of excitement to flying. Up there you've got the entire sky to yourself, the world spread out beneath you. It's incredible. Have you ever been up in a private plane?"

A shudder ran through her body and she shook her head. "No. That's one subject we won't agree on. I'm not a fan of small planes. I have enough trouble getting myself to relax on a commercial flight."

He seemed disappointed. "If you're inferring that light planes aren't safe, they are. It all depends on the experience of the mechanic and the pilot. If you tried it, I guarantee you'd change your mind."

She shrugged. "Maybe."

After what happened three years ago, she'd vowed never to fly in a private plane. But she didn't want to think about that now. The night was too perfect, with the crisp evening breeze, the dark velvet sky, and the frothy tide softly ebbing and flowing just a few yards away.

She turned her head, focusing on the perfect sets of twin footprints they'd left behind in the damp sand. His looked large and solid next to her smaller ones. She thought how wonderful it was to have a man at her side, to walk with, talk with, share with. If only—

Stop it, Desiree, she warned herself. *You know it's impossible.*

She searched quickly for a new topic to divert her mind. "What do you do about traffic lights when you're driving?"

"I can tell by position. Red's always on top. Green's on the bottom."

"I never thought of that."

"It's only a problem when there's a flashing light. I'm never sure if it's red or yellow, so I just plow right through."

She gasped, then realized he was teasing and laughed. "You seem to have adjusted well."

"No, I haven't." He stopped and wrapped his arms around her. "As you saw yesterday, I'm still embarrassed about it."

Her pulse accelerated as her slender body pressed against the solid strength of his. It seemed only natural to slide her own arms around his waist. "Why is it embarrassing?"

"It's a flaw. It means there's something permanently wrong with me. When the leaves turn colors in autumn, I can't see them. The trees all look the same to me. Just plain dull brown."

She wished she had the courage to rub her hands up across his back, to learn the feel of his contoured muscles against the palms of her hands. "It hurts me to think of all the beauty you're missing," she whispered.

He looked down at her, his eyes reflecting the moon-light's glow. "All the beauty I'll ever need to see is right here, in my arms." He raised his hand, and she felt the rough strength of his index finger caress her cheek and trace the curve of her jaw. When his fingertip reached the corner of her lips, he paused, his eyes locking with hers. She read there his admiration, his desire, and his intent.

Desiree's heart seemed first to stop, then beat double time. She shouldn't kiss him. She should step back and deliver her friends-only smile.

But just as moths are drawn to flame, she boldly followed the dictates of her instinct. She stood on her tiptoes, moved her hands to the back of his neck, threaded her fingers through his short hair, and offered her lips to him. Dazed by the fire of need blazing through her veins, she whispered, "Kiss me."

He didn't need a second invitation. His mouth came down on hers in a single expedient motion, the force of his lips matching the depth of passion in her voice.

A moment later, they took a simultaneous, ragged breath, their eyes locked, glimmering with delight in the newness of what they'd just found. She felt his body tremble slightly against hers, as if he were struggling to contain the same impulses raging within her.

"Desiree ...." he whispered.

It was the first time she'd heard him say her name. He whispered it reverently, with the sensual French inflection for which it was intended. It sounded like a prayer.

When his lips met hers again, it was with gentle persuasion. His mouth moved slowly, teasingly over hers, as if savoring her warm softness. She felt her knees weaken beneath the feather-light contact, and he slid his hands tenderly up and down the length of her back, then pulled her more tightly against him.

His tongue flicked back and forth across her lips, then delved into her mouth, hot and insistent. She arched against him, unsure if the rapid thudding she felt against his hard chest was the beating of his heart or her own.

Kyle drew back slightly, then trailed fiery kisses across her cheek and buried his face in her hair at the side of her neck. He heaved an uneven sigh, still holding her against him possessively.

"*You are Desiree.* Desired. Wanted. Longed for." He pulled his head back and brought his wide, firm hands up to cradle her face. "I've wanted to kiss you from the first moment I saw you, standing there like some enchanted sprite in your studio. And when I had you in my arms last night, before we said goodnight ...."

He paused, taking a deep breath as if to steady himself. "I could see you weren't ready, that I was going too fast. I can't tell you how hard it's been to wait, to force myself to keep my hands off you."

"You didn't have to wait long," she whispered.

"Wrong." His lips nuzzled her ear. "We met on the air at three-forty-five yesterday afternoon. That was ... let's see ...." He raised his head, eyes squinting as he made the mental calculation. "Thirty-one hours ago. Believe me, it's been long enough."

He kissed her again, harder this time, then drew back and moved his gaze lingeringly over her face, as if trying to memorize every detail.

A sudden rush of icy water raced up the sand and swirled about their ankles. Desiree squealed as the wave splashed their bare legs with cold salty spray and foam. Kyle grabbed her hand, and they made a dash for higher land.

"Let's go home." He said the word *home* as if it were his home too, a place they both shared. For some reason, she didn't mind. They retraced their steps to his car and drove back to her house, their feet still bare and sandy.

When they arrived, she opened the car door and

gestured toward the house with a nod of her head. "Come on in and get cleaned up. I'll make you a mug of Mexican coffee, my own special recipe."

"Who could refuse an invitation like that?"

They dusted off most of the sand from their feet, then went inside. His eyes widened when they passed through her sparkling-clean living room.

"What happened here in the past twenty-four hours? Did the maid get back from vacation?"

"Spring cleaning," she retorted, grabbing his hand and pulling him down the hall. "Out of season."

"Well, the place looks terrific."

"Don't get too excited. The back half of the house still thinks it's the dead of winter."

She tried to hurry him through to the master bathroom, hoping he wouldn't notice her bedroom's state of disarray. To her dismay, he stopped beside her unmade, four-poster bed, and wrapped one hand around a carved bedpost which reached his chin.

"You weren't kidding," he said. "You've really got one hell of a bed here."

Remembering her remark the day before about her antique headboard, she followed his line of sight. He was paying more attention to the thrown-back comforter and exposed rumpled sheets, however, than to the exquisitely carved mahogany.

She gave him a shove toward the bathroom. "You have no respect for antiques."

"I do. I have a deep and abiding respect for antiques." He yanked back the shower curtain over the porcelain bathtub. "I'm looking at one right here. A pink bathtub! Where would you find a pink bathtub nowadays?"

Her mouth opened and she took a sharp breath, watching him closely. Should she tell him? The bathtub was green. She closed her mouth again.

"You're right," she said. "You hardly ever see pink anymore."

He seemed unaware of his mistake or her reaction to it, and she was glad. Quirking a brow in her direction he asked, "Want to take a bath?"

"No!" She tried to sound irritated and failed miserably. She handed him a washcloth and towel from the linen closet and turned on the water in the tub. "I'm going to rinse my feet off. Or do you want to go first?"

"No, please. Be my guest."

Standing alongside the tub, she dipped one foot under the running water. Bending forward, she washed the sand from between her toes and then switched legs. She was halfway through before she realized what a view her too-brief cutoffs must be providing Kyle. She jerked upright and whirled around.

"Don't mind me." The glimmer in his eyes made her cheeks flush red-hot.

"I'm done. I'll just wait for you in the other room." Desiree grabbed her towel and escaped out the door, her feet dripping as she ran.

∽

"THAT WAS DELICIOUS." Kyle finished the last of the coffee she'd laced with tequila and a generous dollop of cream. "I don't get Mexican coffee too often up in Seattle."

She sat beside him on the living-room couch, her bare feet, now clean and dry, tucked beneath her. "A definite drawback to being a northerner."

"There are other drawbacks I can think of." Putting down his cup, he drew her into his arms, his lips against her hair. "I had a great time tonight."

"So did I."

He held her against him for a moment, then bent his head and pressed his lips lightly against hers. He smoothed her cheek with his fingertips and kissed her again, and again, lingering longer with each soft touch of his mouth on hers.

A cloud of desire enveloped her, wrapping her in its swirling depths. She wanted to give in to her body's yearning, to press herself against his hard strength and let his body imbue her with warmth.

But red warning lights started flashing in the corners of her mind, reminding her of the reasons she'd been wary of going out with him in the first place.

Gripping his shoulders lightly, she said, "Wait. Kyle. We should—"

"Should what?"

"Say good-night. You're going home tomorrow, and—"

"Am I?" He brushed his lips against hers. "That depends on you."

"On me?"

He nodded, drawing back slightly. "I'll be tied up in a meeting all day tomorrow, but I'm in no rush to fly home.

We've got Friday night and the whole weekend ahead of us. If you'll let me see you again, if you want me to stay … I'll be here until the last possible second. Until Monday morning at dawn."

Surprise and confusion rendered her speechless. Her heart began to pound.

He searched her face for an answer. "Do you want me to stay?"

He took advantage of her moment of hesitation to lower his mouth back to hers. His hands roved across her shoulders, then tenderly massaged her back before sliding around to brush the sides of her breasts.

She tried to resist. She couldn't. Melting against him, she lifted her arms to caress his neck, her fingertips lacing through the thick short waves of his hair.

His mouth moved slowly, gently against hers, his kiss kindling a fire that burst into flame deep within her. His tongue circled hers, exploring, dipping deeper, deeper, as if searching for each hidden sweet taste.

He turned, lowering her gently onto the sofa. His hand caressed first one breast and then the other through the thin fabric of her shirt and bra. A thousand tiny explosions coursed through her. Her entire body began to throb with sexual awareness, from her breasts, so full and aching, to an exquisite mounting tension between her thighs.

A moan escaped her lips. He lowered his body on top of hers and recaptured her mouth in a deep burning kiss. She felt the evidence of his arousal, hard and insistent against her. It only intensified her desire. *Make love to me*, her body sang out at the same time as her mind shouted, *No!*

With the last vestige of her self-control, she tore her mouth from his.

"Kyle," she gasped. "This is all happening so fast. I haven't known you long enough. I—"

"I feel as if I've known you all my life," he said huskily. His palm caressed her cheek, gently urging her to meet his warm gaze. This time there was another, more immediate meaning in the question he whispered feverishly in her ear.

"Do you want me to stay?"

CHAPTER 5

N-no." Desiree pulled herself out of his arms and jumped to her feet, her fingers trembling as they fumbled to straighten her T-shirt.

Kyle sat up on the couch and leaned forward, resting his forearms on his thighs, hands clasped together. For a while he stared at the plush area rug beneath their feet, taking slow, deep breaths, as if struggling to regain his composure.

His words, when he spoke, sounded clipped, yet still congenial. "Do you mean *no,* you don't want me to stay the weekend, or *no,* you don't want me to spend the night?"

Desiree turned toward the fireplace and stared at the dark, lifeless hearth, her fingers tightly interlaced to stop them from shaking: What was she doing? She'd wanted to go out with Kyle, there was no denying it, but she'd promised herself not to get ... *involved* with him. How could she have let things get so out of hand?

"No ... to both questions," she replied, her voice tremulous.

His head whipped up. "What?"

She faced him again. "There's no need for you to change your plans to go back to Seattle. I'm really sorry, but ...." She swallowed hard, forcing herself to continue. "I won't be able to see you tomorrow."

His forehead furrowed in a puzzled frown. "Why not? Don't you get off at six?"

"Yes. But I have to work late."

"How late?"

"There are a bunch of commercials I have to produce. It might take hours. I have to put music behind them, do the vocals, cut them onto tape, record them on cart—"

"Cart?"

"Short for cartridge," she explained impatiently. "I should have done it tonight, but—"

"Okay," he conceded. "I get it. You're busy tomorrow night. What about Saturday?"

"I have to work all day. All weekend, in fact."

"All weekend?" He stared at her. "What kind of a schedule is that? You must get off sometime?"

"I just got this new shift," she said evasively. "The schedule's not final yet."

He stood up, shoved his hands in his pockets, the muscles in his forearms rigid and distended. "I see."

Guiltily, she lowered her gaze. Her hands ached to touch his cheek, his neck, his arms. Her lips yearned for the feel of his mouth on hers again, the taste of his tongue encircling hers.

But she knew if he took her in his arms again, if she gave herself up to the thrill of his tantalizing caresses, all her willpower would fly out the window. He'd end up spending the night.

And she couldn't do that. Once she'd made love to Kyle, she sensed that her heart would never be able to let him go.

She took several steps back. An unpleasant shiver ran up her legs as her bare feet left the cozy warmth of the area rug and came in contact with the cold, hardwood floor.

"Thank you for the ice cream and the walk on the beach, Kyle. It was wonderful. And thank you again for the roses. I—"

"Desiree." The deep, resonant timbre in his voice made her jump. "Stop talking as if this is goodbye. If you're busy this weekend, I understand. I'll call you when I get home. We'll pick another weekend. I'll fly back down."

"No." Her back struck the credenza and she froze as he took a step toward her. "I'm glad I met you, Kyle. I really am. But I think it's better if we end things here. I told you before, I can't get involved with you ... with anyone."

He crossed the room in two strides and stopped before her. "We're already involved."

"We can't be. We shouldn't be. You live too far away. It's —" Her voice broke and she turned her head to avoid his heated gaze. "It's just going to cause a lot of heartache for both of us."

"What if it does? I can stand a little heartache, can't you? Isn't it better than not feeling at all?"

She opened her mouth to respond, then closed it, unable to utter her intended denial.

"Desiree, I've been alone a long time. I'm sick of it. There's something special between us. And I'm not just talking about physical desire. I felt it the first moment I saw you, and I'm certain of it now."

One arm swept down to the small of her back and he cradled her against his chest, then lowered his face to hers. She stiffened slightly, struggling to maintain her resolve despite the warm glow of desire that rekindled within her body each time it came into contact with his.

"I felt you respond to me," he said. "I feel you responding now. You want me as much as I want you. Admit it."

She squeezed her eyes shut, trying to block out the fiery eyes and sensuous lips so dangerously close to her own. She wanted to say No, but all she managed was: "Kyle, I—"

He cut off her next words with the pressure of his lips. His hands traveled across her back, up and down her spine, sending rockets of desire shuttling to uncharted regions of her body.

Desiree's mind reeled. The throbbing in her chest spread down toward her loins, where it pulsed a frenzied rhythm.

The tiny part of her that could still think told her to break away from his embrace. But her body acted of its own volition. Her arms wrapped around his back. Her fingers grasped his shoulder blades, pulling him closer. She molded her body against his lean, muscled frame.

At her response he moaned, low and deep in his throat. Apparently sensing she'd resist no further, he relaxed his hold, took a ragged breath, and began to move his lips slowly, gently, persuasively over hers.

His fingertips stroked through the silky hair at her nape. His warm, sweet breath fanned her mouth as his feathery kisses tickled and teased her lips, then brushed across her cheeks, nose, and jaw.

She felt her limbs melt like candle wax against a flame as he again lowered his mouth to drop a series of long, sensuous kisses along her neck and throat.

Her breathing was short and shallow and she leaned her head back to allow him full access to her throat. She held him tighter, no longer certain her quaking legs could support her weight.

Ever so slowly he kissed his way back up her neck, across her cheek to her forehead. Then, tenderly, he folded her in his arms and brought her head down against his chest.

Silently, he held her.

Even if she had wanted to push herself away from him, there wasn't strength left in her limbs. Her cheek lay against the softness of his shirt, and she could feel his chest, moving up and down in an erratic rhythm against hers as they caught their breath.

He was right; there was no denying the attraction she felt for him, and it seemed that he felt the same way. But what exactly did he want from her? A weekend fling? Someone to keep his bed warm on his business trips down south? Or did he imagine there could be more to it than that?

She knew that any kind of future between them was extremely unlikely, if not impossible. His home, his work was in Seattle, and hers was here. She knew what it was like to be separated from the one you loved.

She'd never forget the loneliness of those long months without Steve, longing for his company at the end of each day, reaching out for him in the empty darkness at night. No matter who was to blame, she'd learned her lesson. If she wanted a career in radio, she had to remain free and independent. She couldn't give her heart to any man.

"Kyle," she said, fingering the lapel of his shirt as she looked up at him, "I can't hide the way I feel about you. But I tried to explain last night—there's no way a relationship can work between us."

"I heard what you said last night. Every word. Your lack of job security, the way you have to move every few years, all the excuses you've learned to cling to as reasons not to get involved with anyone. So, you might get fired any minute, so what? We already live a thousand miles apart. What difference would another few miles make?"

All the difference in the world, she wanted to say. But she didn't want to dredge up the painful memories she'd managed to bury so deep inside her. Still, somehow, she had to make him see.

"One of us will end up getting hurt," she whispered. "I know it."

"You can't know that." He kissed her again, long and hard. "I'm not trying to predict how things will end up between us, Desiree. But let's give it a chance. Let's take things one day at a time. If it's meant to be, it will be. I've waited a long time to find you, and I'm not about to give you up now."

A BIRD CHIRPED outside Desiree's window. She opened her eyes and squinted against the first faint light of a grey dawn. She must have finally dozed off. How many hours did she toss and turn last night, thoughts of Kyle and his impassioned caresses burning into her mind, keeping sleep at bay?

Even now, her mind still spun with confusion. Why wouldn't he listen to her? Why, when he left, did he insist that she would hear from him again?

Why did that make her feel like shouting for joy?

It didn't seem possible that they'd only met two days before. Nothing seemed the same. Her room, cast in shadows by the unfamiliar early-morning light, looked foreign to her. Her bed, which had always seemed so warm and inviting beneath the fluffy white comforter, had never felt so hard ... so cold ... or so empty.

Her response to Kyle's embraces filled her with equal measures of fear and exhilaration. No man's touch had ever inspired in her such fierce desire.

And what she felt was more than just a physical response. She enjoyed being with him, loved the sound of his voice, the knack he had of putting her at ease, the way he laughed at her jokes. In only two days he'd made her feel more beautiful, more feminine, and more desirable than she'd ever felt in her life.

With the slightest encouragement, she could easily fall in love with him. And to do that ... well, history had a way of repeating itself, and she knew *that* could only end badly.

What on earth was she going to do?

With a sigh, she threw back the covers and climbed out of bed. For now, there was nothing she *could* do. He'd left without saying when he'd call, or if he intended to stop by.

She'd told him she'd be busy all weekend, so presumably he'd return to Seattle tonight. Or would he?

She went into the bathroom and stepped beneath the shower's warm, stinging spray. The morning sped by as she straightened up her bedroom, paid a few bills, and watered the flower beds in her front yard.

She showed up at the station with an hour to spare, produced three commercials in record time, and slipped into her seat at the console at precisely two o'clock. She was more than halfway through her shift, standing by her counter logging promos, when Barbara threw open the door.

"Hi, Des. What's new with my—" Barbara pulled to an abrupt halt in the doorway and stared at Desiree, her eyes wide. "What are you wearing?"

Desiree shot an impatient glance over her shoulder. "It's quite obvious what I'm wearing."

"But it's a ... *skirt!*" Barbara uttered the word in disbelief, as if a skirt were the last thing on earth a thirty-year-old female would wear.

Desiree smoothed the folds of her floral wrap-around over her knees and fluffed the ruffled V-neckline of her sleeveless turquoise blouse. She'd bought the outfit months ago, even though she had nowhere special to wear it. "You act like you've never seen a skirt before," she said testily.

"I haven't—not on you. Since the day we met, you've worn nothing but cutoffs or jeans. What's the occasion? You must be going somewhere."

Barbara's glance darted to the vase of roses which still graced the counter beside the console, and her eyes widened in understanding. "You're seeing Kyle Harrison, aren't you?" She grinned. "Far be it from me to say I told you so." Without waiting for an answer, she flounced out the door.

Desiree had barely a moment to process her frustration over this encounter when the door opened again and Tom poked his head inside. "I had to see it for myself. Oh my God, it's true. You *are* wearing a skirt."

"Get out of here!" Desiree glared at him.

Tom shook his head. "For two years I've offered up my body on a plate, and who do you fall for? Some loser in a rented Maserati."

Desiree picked up a paperback and hurled it at him. The door slammed just in time.

She climbed up on the stool, put on her headphones, and drummed her fingernails against the console, waiting for her cue.

"102 FM, KICK on this Friday afternoon," she said into the mike. "That was Kenny Rogers with 'Why Was I So Blind?' from his latest album 'Cutting Loose.' The weekend's almost upon us now and we'll all be cutting loose. It's ten minutes before five o'clock."

She played three more songs, then ran a commercial break. She began to read a public service announcement about the annual aerobics dance for the National Heart Association when she heard the studio door quietly open yet again behind her.

She froze. *No one* would dare to walk in here when the red light was on, while she was live on the air. No one, that is, except ....

"You can win some exciting prizes," she said, trying to keep her voice steady as she read, "get some great exercise, and have a whole lot of fun." She heard the door shut with an almost silent click.

"Sign up now. That's the Dance for Your Heart ...."

Strong hands came to rest on her shoulder blades. Warm lips pressed against her neck. She stifled a gasp as a frenzied shiver traveled up her spine.

"... at the Anaheim Convention Center ...."

Strong hands rove up and down her bare arms. A heady languor descended over her, as if her veins were flowing with thick, sweet syrup. Her voice slowed and deepened with each touch of his fingers.

"... next Saturday, June twenty-seventh." Her chest rose and fell with increasing rapidity as his mouth nuzzled against her throat. Her ears began to pound. She strained to hear her own voice.

"For registration forms, call the National Heart Association." She read off the phone number. "Or stop by the studio at KICK."

Desiree flicked off the mike and punched a button on the cart deck to start the next song. Pulling off her headphones, she heaved a sigh of relief. Familiar arms swept around her mid-section and pulled her back against a masculine frame.

"I missed you," Kyle said against her ear, his voice soft and deep.

"Don't you know what a red warning light is?" She tried to sound indignant, but the words came out like a soft sigh.

"Yes," he murmured. "It's the signal that flashes in my brain every time I see you."

She leaned her head back against his shoulder and closed her eyes, enveloped by his warmth and the spicy scent of his cologne. "I'm talking about the big red beacon on the wall outside the control-room door."

He lifted his head. "Red? You mean that green light telling me it's all right to come in?"

She gasped, remembering he was color blind. "Oh! You thought it was green?" But when she turned around to look at him, she saw a flash of devilment in his eyes. "Liar!"

He laughed. "I assumed it was red. I know what a warning light means."

"Then why did you—"

"Barbara said it was okay—just like last time—as long as I was quiet. And I wanted to surprise you."

"Well," she huffed, "you succeeded. But don't ever do that again. The mike picks up every little sound."

He leaned over and breathed close to her ear. "Every little sound?"

"Yes."

"Would it pick up this sound?" He kissed the side of her neck.

Her head tilted upward, as if obeying a silent command. "Yes," she said huskily.

"And this?" He dropped kisses around the graceful curve of her neck to the hollow of her throat.

"Definitely."

"Then I guess I'll have to restrain myself while we're in here."

"You will. Otherwise, I might make a mistake. Say the wrong thing. Sound totally off."

"*Au contraire.* I'll wager you've never sounded more sultry or sensuous in your life than you did on the air just now. I only helped promote your image."

"I've been doing just fine on my own, thank you." Desiree knew she was playing with fire. This time her job, not just her emotions, were on the line.

Anyone might walk by and see them through the windows. If Sam caught them kissing, or if she missed so much as one precious cue, his rage would be immediate and intense.

She slipped off the stool and stepped aside. "I guess you missed your flight to Seattle?"

"Looks that way. Pity, isn't it?" He leaned back against the counter, his eyes sliding the length of her slim figure. He whistled. "Don't you look nice. Quite a change from your previous work attire."

Her cheeks grew hot. "I felt like dressing up a little today."

"Just in case I decided to stop by?"

"No!" She pushed him out of her way. "Because I felt like it." With a glance at the rotation chart, she cued up the next few songs.

"Whatever the reason, I'm glad you did. I figured we'd need time for you to go home and change, but now we can fit in a quick dinner before the show if we leave right at six."

"Dinner?" Her glance fell on his wrists, where square, gold cuff links glimmered in the cuffs of his long-sleeved dress shirt. He wore the light grey suit she remembered from the night they met, this time with a matching vest. "Show?" she asked.

He pulled two theater tickets out of his breast pocket and handed them to her. "I had a hell of a time getting these."

She stared at the tickets in astonishment. They were for a new musical that had gotten rave reviews. "This show has been sold out for months."

"So they told me. I badgered them so long at the box office, though, they finally managed to find something. I hope you can go? Last night, I know you said you had to work late …."

She smiled sheepishly. "As luck would have it, my schedule just opened up." She slid the tickets back into his jacket pocket. "Thank you for getting these. I've been dying to see this show."

"So have I. It'll be even more fun to see it together."

She couldn't argue with that. Her attention returned briefly to her work as the song on the air ended with a cold fade. She expertly segued into the next tune.

Kyle's eyes darted about the room, finally coming to rest on the row of knobs, meters, and buttons on her console. "Correct me if I'm wrong, but this equipment isn't exactly state of the art, is it?"

She shook her head and touched a hand to one of the black knobs. "No. Most control boards today have levers instead of pots like these."

"Pots?"

"Short for potentiometer. It controls the level of modulation. There are usually remote starts right in a row, so the operator doesn't have to go through as many motions." She smiled ruefully. "Lucky me. With all the new equipment around today, I end up at a station with an ancient system."

"But this is a major market. From what I've read, you're a highly rated station in Orange County. Why doesn't the owner modernize?"

"This place is only a hobby for him. He owns several other companies that keep him busy, and he has some pretty definite ideas about what to spend his money on. The equipment works, he says. As long as we have an engineer who knows how to keep it running, he'll make it last for ages." She shrugged. "He'd rather spend his money on an air watch pilot, if you can believe that."

"An air watch pilot? You mean you have your own man in a plane up there?"

She nodded. "I'll show you. Traffic is next. Hang on."

She whipped on her headphones and turned up the volume inside the studio for Kyle's benefit, then switched on the mike. "It's five o'clock. You've got Desiree, and this is KICK-FM, Anaheim. Now let's hear from our daredevil in the skies, Deadly Dave Dawson." She punched a button marked Traffic on the control board. "Dave?"

"Hey, Desiree. You were breathing pretty hard a few minutes ago. Who've you got in there with you? Some hot, young stud?"

She felt a blush start in her cheeks and spread to the roots of her hair. This was their typical daily banter. Dave was always kidding her about the sensual quality of her voice. How was he to know that this particular time his comment hit the nail on the head?

"The truth is, Dave, I do have somebody in here." She turned and met Kyle's amused gaze. "He's incredibly rich, devilishly handsome, has a fantastic body, and the most gorgeous green eyes you've ever seen."

"Oh yeah? Who is this mystery man?"

"That's *my* little secret." Out of the comer of her eye, she saw the buttons light up on her phone. Don't miss a trick, do they? she thought with a grin. "Now what about that traffic? How's it look out there?"

A chuckle traveled the airwaves. "Things aren't looking *too* bad for a Friday night. The Golden State southbound is slow and go at ...."

As Dave continued the traffic report, Desiree's earphones were plucked from her head and an arm stole around her again from behind. Quickly she flipped off the mike.

"Devilishly handsome?" he murmured, his lips against her ear. "Fantastic body? Gorgeous eyes?"

"I guess I did get a little carried away." As she sat on the stool, his chest pressed against her back, she couldn't stop her eyes from closing and her neck from arching back and resting against his shoulder. "As long as they *think* someone's in here, let's give them something to worry about."

"Great idea." He slowly rotated the stool until her side rested against him. Cupping her chin in his hand, he turned her mouth up to his and tantalized it with light, soft kisses. His free hand roamed to her opposite hip, holding her captive against his chest as his tongue traced her lips, then slipped inside her mouth.

She returned the kiss as it became deeper, locking her hands behind his neck and pulling him closer. In the back of her mind, she heard a voice, distorted words, droning on in what seemed a foreign language.

"Stalled vehicle ... 605 northbound ... no other problems ...."

She was spinning, as if from lack of oxygen, as if Kyle was drawing the breath from her body.

"That's about it for ..." The voice hazily penetrated her

dazed state. The words formed a familiar pattern, then began to flash in her brain like a neon sign. "... Dawson for KICK. Have a nice weekend."

Desiree bolted upright, pushed Kyle away with a shaky hand and turned up the volume control on the console. Her heart pounded in her ears as, with several instinctive, expedient motions, she started the next tune and sank back against the counter, arms hanging limply at her sides.

Glancing quickly out the control room window in both directions, she confirmed that, thankfully, there was no one in sight. "Kyle. How do you expect me to do my job, when you ...."

"When I what?"

"When you hold me and kiss me like that!"

He lifted his palms, shrugging innocently. "Sorry."

She attempted to glare at him, but suspected she was failing miserably. "I can't concentrate with you in here. Go sit out in the waiting area until I'm finished. Go!"

With a smile, he moved to the door. "Six o'clock," he reminded her. "I'll be waiting."

DESIREE RELAXED against the contoured leather seat of the Maserati and closed her eyes. The engine hummed a soft lullaby, blending harmoniously with the colorful kaleidoscope of images floating through her mind.

"I didn't think anyone could tap dance so fast," she murmured.

"Neither did I," Kyle said, chuckling. "What a show."

She couldn't remember ever spending a more enjoyable

evening. They'd feasted on a delectable *canard a l'orange* at a small, French restaurant near the theater. Kyle, recalling that duck with orange sauce and *salade Lyonnaise*—a classic salad that featured baby frisée, bacon, a poached egg, and croutons tossed with a Dijon vinaigrette—were two of Desiree's favorite dishes, had ordered everything in advance, including another one of her favorites, a delicious *tart aux pommes* for dessert.

He'd arranged for the meal to be served with a minimum of delay, and they'd arrived at the Music Center in downtown Los Angeles just minutes before the show began.

The musical was an extravaganza of dazzling costumes and breathtaking production numbers. But even the star's spectacular toe-tapping could not compare with the thrill and pride she'd felt just being in Kyle's company.

Other women had stared at him as they'd walked by, and no wonder. In his perfectly tailored suit and silk tie, his hair carefully groomed, and his face recently shaved, he looked handsome, sophisticated, and indisputably masculine.

The mind-stealing embraces they'd shared earlier in the studio, made all the more exciting by their illicit nature, had never strayed from her thoughts. During the show, when his hand had reached over to gently warm her thigh through the thin fabric of her skirt, it had required rigorous self-control to keep her breathing steady and focus on the stage.

But now, although he sat just inches from her in the cozy interior of the small sportscar and his hand brushed her cheek tenderly, she felt too relaxed and content to be aroused.

"I couldn't believe it when he tapped his way up and down that entire staircase," he murmured.

Drowsily, she caressed his hand. "That *was* amazing. Like something out of a Fred Astaire movie." She opened her eyes and smiled. "Thank you again for getting the tickets."

He squeezed her shoulder. "Any time."

They drove along in contented, companionable silence. The effects of Desiree's sleepless night and hectic day finally caught up with her, and she drifted off. It seemed only minutes later that she heard the engine clicking off and the car's final shudder into silent stillness.

Disoriented, she tried to speak, but only managed a small yawn. All at once she felt herself being gathered up by a pair of strong arms as warm lips pressed against hers.

"Wake up, sleepyhead," he whispered. "We're home."

"Already?" She slowly opened her eyes.

Moonlight splashed through the windshield, making her squint. The silvery beam that bathed her face only touched the side of his cheek, illuminating its smooth, angular planes in an intriguing display of half-light, half-shadow.

"You've been asleep for half an hour." He leaned back slightly and threaded his fingers through her hair. "Did anyone ever tell you that you're beautiful when you're asleep? Even more beautiful than when you're awake, if that's possible."

"You're just saying that because it's true," she mumbled.

He laughed, his eyes inky black in the darkness.

His nearness, his warmth, and his unique masculine scent enveloped her senses. Kiss me again, she wanted to plead. But as she lifted her hand to touch his cheek, a sudden, inexplicable shyness came over her.

She lowered her eyes, let her hand fall away, and toyed with the edge of the smooth leather seat, struggling to make conversation. "This is such a nice car. I've been meaning to ask ... where do you rent a Maserati?"

"There's a place near the airport." With measured slowness, his thumb traced small, sensuous circles at the side of her neck.

She caught her breath. Could he feel the erratic pulse beating beneath the pad of his thumb?

"They have every luxury car you can think of," he added, moving closer. "Rolls-Royce. Mercedes. Ferrari."

"What about ... a Cadillac limousine?"

"Absolutely." His breath fanned her lips. "Limos are their mainstay."

"I've always wanted to ride in a limo."

"Have you?"

"An incredibly long, plush limo, with a built-in bar and a TV."

"An intriguing fantasy. Just think what we could do in a limo."

His mouth pressed tenderly against hers, infusing her body with warmth. His tongue persuaded her lips apart, then probed her mouth, performing an intimate mating dance with her tongue.

As his hands scaled her back, she locked her arms behind his neck, twisted her hands in his hair. She felt a thread of trust weave between them, through them, around them, as if entwining them together for eternity.

"Desiree, you taste so sweet .…"

His hand traced up her side to lightly graze the side of her breast, and her head fell back. A sigh of ecstasy echoed in the night as his lips moved slowly, sensuously up her throat, then covered her mouth once more.

Suddenly he winced sharply, and she felt him draw back.

"What's wrong?" she asked breathlessly.

"I think the stick shift is permanently embedded in my side."

"Oh. I'm sorry."

"And the windshield is all fogged up."

"So is my brain." She laughed softly. "I guess there's no point in kissing out in the car, is there? Would you like to come in for a brandy?"

He leaned his forehead against hers and smiled into her eyes. "I thought you'd never ask."

CHAPTER 6

As Desiree retrieved a bottle of brandy from her credenza and poured two snifters, she watched Kyle take off his tailored suit jacket and hang it neatly over the back of her wingback chair.

His tie soon joined the jacket, and he opened the top two buttons of his shirt.

"That's better." Exhaling deeply, he sank back into the couch. "Ever try to kiss a woman with a tie digging into your neck?"

Desiree laughed. "Not recently." She handed Kyle his drink and sat down next to him.

"Thanks." He raised the glass in a toast. "To the loveliest deejay I've ever met."

"*The* loveliest? How many deejays have you met?"

His lips tilted up in a roguish grin. "Not many. And all the others were men."

"That's what I thought. Thanks a lot."

"Allow me to amend my toast. To my new favorite deejay. May she forever rule the air waves."

"I'll drink to that." She clinked her glass against his.

He extended an arm across the back of the couch, his eyes caressing her face as he slowly sipped his brandy.

"I hope you know ...." His voice dropped to a husky whisper. "I was proud to be out with you tonight. Not just because you're lovely to look at, but because you're ... you."

Her heart hammered in her chest as she drank in his frankly adoring gaze for a long, heady moment. She'd been told she was beautiful before. She'd never once believed it. Hearing the words on his lips made her *feel* beautiful for the first time in her life.

Her heart soared. She wanted to respond in kind, tell him how attractive she found him and how much she enjoyed his company, but before she could voice her thoughts, he said:

"You mentioned that you were married once. Will you tell me about it? What happened?"

Tearing her eyes from his gaze, she stared into the amber liquid in her glass. "It's not a happy memory. It was over five years ago, but I still have scars. To tell you the truth, I'd rather not talk about it."

He took the glass from her hand and set it on the coffee table. The arm behind her dropped to her shoulders and his other hand cupped her face, tilting it gently up to his. "Did he hurt you?" His jaw tensed. "Because if he did ...."

"No. Not in the way you mean. My scars are purely emotional. I don't blame him for wanting the divorce. It wasn't entirely his fault. Mostly it was mine."

"I doubt that. He'd have to be an idiot to give you up."

His lips met hers, both possessive and gentle at the same time. His arms wrapped around her tenderly, adoringly. Her arms encircled his back as she relished the taste of him, the heat of his skin, the silken texture of his hair.

"Desiree …." His lips now nibbled the length of her throat, then took small, teasing bites from her earlobe. "All night, I've been dying to hold you … kiss you … touch you like this."

His mouth returned to hers as his hand closed over the fullness of her breast. Slowly he rotated his fingers and palm until her desire bubbled within his grasp. His other hand pulled her blouse loose from the waistband of her skirt and slid up her back.

His hand felt rough and masculine against her smooth, bare flesh, sending tingles up her spine. Slowly he stood up, pulling her with him, and held her against his chest.

His hand glided past her waist, to cup the soft swell of her buttocks. He pressed her body against his, making her aware of his desire. Even through the layers of their clothing she could feel the rapid drumming of his heart, which beat in cadence with her own.

"You told me last night you didn't want to see me again, that you didn't want me," he whispered against her lips. "Did you mean it? Was it true?"

His eyes were shining with affection, alive with need. She tried to tell herself that this was wrong, that they shouldn't go any further, that she *didn't* want him. Instead, she admitted, "No. It wasn't true."

Without another word, he swept her up into his arms. She felt his mouth against her forehead, her cheek, her hair. His footsteps echoed on the hardwood floor as he carried her down the dark hallway.

This shouldn't be happening, she thought helplessly, as she wrapped her arms around him and buried her face against his neck. But she didn't want to stop it. Did she?

He nudged open the door to her bedroom with his foot and strode inside, lowering her gently onto the bed. She heard him fumble with the bedside lamp, then a flick of the switch and the room was filled with soft, golden light.

As if in a dream, she watched him shrug out of his vest and toss it onto a nearby chair, then sit down on the edge of the bed and take off his shoes.

Still wearing his shirt and pants, he turned toward her and grasped her foot, pulling off first one sandal and then the other. He cradled one of her feet in his hands, massaged the high arch, circled his thumb over her toes.

"Such tiny feet," he said with wonder. "So delicate. And your legs ... they're beautiful." His hand slid up one bare calf, under her skirt to cup her knee. His touch sent flames licking up her thighs.

Don't do this, warned a voice inside her head. She pulled herself upright on the bed, her body stiff with uncertainty, her pulse racing.

"Kyle," she began.

"You know how I feel about you." He gently pulled her down on the bed next to him, held her against the length of his body. "I've made no secret of it." His voice dropped to a husky whisper. "Am I reading something that isn't there? Or do you feel the same way about me?"

"You know I do," she whispered.

"Then let me show you how much I care. Let me make love to you."

"I'm not sure it's right for me, for either of us. This is all happening too fast."

"It *is* happening fast. I never imagined it could be this way. But that doesn't mean it isn't right." His hand stroked her cheek as he gazed lovingly into her eyes. "There's nothing more beautiful than what we feel for each other right now."

Right now. His words drummed in her head, bringing to the surface all her reservations, all her fears.

Right now. For the moment.

Temporary. Temporary insanity.

Catching the look in her eyes, he said softly, "We can stop right now if you want. It's up to you. But help me to understand. What are you afraid of?"

Of you. Of me. That I'll fall in love with you, and when it's time to say goodbye, I'll never recover. She couldn't make love to a man without giving her heart and her soul, and she was already perilously close to giving both to Kyle.

Monday morning you'll be gone, she thought, and I'll be left empty and aching.

She wanted to tell him, to try to explain, but her throat felt so constricted she couldn't speak.

"You said the other night that you'll never get married again, that your divorce was inevitable. Aren't you being a little hard on yourself? Are you so afraid of failure that you won't allow yourself to love anyone again?"

She closed her eyes. "That's ... part of it," she managed.

"Have you been with anyone since then?"

She shook her head. Unbidden tears sprang into her eyes. He smoothed her hair back and kissed away her tears. "Don't be afraid, Desiree. We can never be certain what the future holds for us. But don't let that stop you from living, from loving."

The tears brimmed over and trickled down her cheeks.

"Don't cry, my darling. Don't cry." His lips moved across her eyes, cheeks, and chin, and brushed away her tears, absorbing them into his own mouth. "Oh, God, Desiree, I'm sorry."

He stretched out on his side and cuddled her close against him, massaging her back and heaving long, steadying breaths as if fighting to regain control over his body.

Finally, his voice deep and vibrant, he said, "I didn't mean to push you into something you're not ready for. I'm sorry. I don't want to hurt you, my darling. I only want to love you."

My darling. A shuddering sigh escaped her control. No one had ever called her my darling. Not even Steve. Until this moment, she didn't realize how much she'd always longed to hear just those words, in just the way he had said them.

Her arms looped around his back. Her hands tangled in his hair. Oh, Kyle, she thought. I didn't want to need you. I didn't want to want you. But I can't help myself. I do. Her eyes met his with a wordless plea, revealing the depth of her emotions and desire as she tilted her lips up to his.

He read her assent in her gaze. With a low moan, he rolled on top of her. His lips touched hers again, with such sensitivity and gentle adoration it took her breath away.

His tongue slid between her lips, then encircled hers with a slow, tender intimacy. His hands roamed over her shoulders, then down to caress her breasts through her silky blouse.

She felt herself relax beneath him. All her reasons to

resist drifted away to some dark, forgotten corner of her mind. It's going to be all right, she told herself. Somehow, he'll make it right.

His hand reached down to unbutton her blouse, and when he reached inside her lacy bra to cup her breast, a shudder of pleasure rocketed through her and she called his name out loud.

He raised her up slowly and slid the blouse and wispy bra from her body. At his sharp intake of breath, she felt her heart begin to pound.

"You're perfect," he said huskily.

He laid her back down and kissed her as his hand covered one breast, fingers stroking gently, seeking to please. His touch sent tiny jolts of electricity through her, like sparks on a live wire.

Her hands roamed across his back, then tugged feverishly at his shirt until it pulled free of his waistband. She ran exploring fingers along the bare, smooth skin above his waist, then traced the distinct ridge in the center of his back.

"I want to see you," she whispered. With quivering fingers, she reached around to grasp the placket of his shirt.

"Let me help you." He sat up, quickly removed the unwanted barrier between them, and let it drop to the floor.

Her heart beat faster as she gazed at his naked chest. Dark, curly hair covered the taut contours of his upper pectorals, then descended in crisp swirls down the center to a thin, tapering line that disappeared into his pants.

She lifted hesitant fingers to his smooth skin, then

SYRIE JAMES

plowed through his soft chest hair. She sensed a barely leashed passion burning beneath the surface of his skin, and it matched the fire raging beneath her own.

He slid down on the bed and enclosed the pointed crown of one breast in his mouth. One hand pushed open the front fold of her wraparound skirt and his fingers glided up her thigh, massaging a path along its inner, most sensitive parts. Her legs began to tremble. His fingers reached the edge of her panties and toyed with the lacy elastic.

"Yes," she breathed.

"Are you sure?" he asked softly.

"I'm sure."

"What about … do I need to—?"

She felt heat rise to her cheeks. "It's okay." She'd been on the Pill for years for health reasons, and she told him so.

He nodded. As she lifted her hips to help him, he slid her panties down along her legs, over her feet. He untied the wraparound skirt at her waist, then drew the folds apart.

"You take my breath away." His voice was as rough as sandpaper.

He stretched up over her and fastened his mouth to hers in a fiery kiss. The pressure and texture of his hard, wiry-haired chest against the sensitive tips of her breasts sent ripples of exquisite sensation throughout her body.

His hand stroked up the inside of her thigh, ever closer to the center of her femininity. A soft moan of desire escaped her throat.

The phone rang.

Their bodies stiffened at the same moment. He lifted his head.

"Don't answer it," he advised.

She lay frozen beneath him. The ring persisted. She glanced at the bedside dock. It was almost midnight. "Who could it be at this hour?"

"Does it matter?" He softly trailed his fingertips along her collarbone.

She took a deep breath, trying desperately to think despite the fire raging throughout her system. "No one would call so late unless it was really important." She turned sideways and reached for the phone. With a groan he rolled off her.

"Hello?" Her voice was as unsteady as her hand.

"Desiree? Thank God you're home." She recognized the gravelly voice of Sam, her program director at the station. "The Board Op just called and got me out of bed. He said John's stuck on the freeway. There's a tow truck on the way, but he doesn't know what time he'll get there. Dave's already worked two shifts and can only stay another half hour. I need you to substitute until John makes it in."

"This isn't a good time. Did you try Mark or Wayne?"

"Wayne's too drunk to stand up straight, and I wasn't able to reach Mark or anyone else."

"I'm sorry Sam, but I can't go in now."

"Dammit, Desiree, don't give me any excuses. If you don't do this, we're dead in the water. You're the only one I can depend upon."

She let out a deep sigh of frustration. "Okay. Fine. I'll be there as soon as I can." She hung up the phone and slid from the bed, her limbs still trembling.

"What is it?"

"The night-shift deejay has car trouble." She explained what happened as she quickly got dressed.

Kyle cursed and sat up on the edge of the bed.

"I'm really sorry," she said sincerely. "I have no choice."

"I know. I understand." He bent down and retrieved his shirt from where it lay on the floor. "Would it help if I drive you to the station and wait for you, so you don't have to drive home alone in the middle of the night?"

"Thanks, but I'll be okay." She struggled to steady both her breathing and her nerves as she fished in her closet for a pair of sandals.

"Then I'll wait for you here." He put on his shirt and began to fasten the buttons.

"No." She swallowed hard, avoiding his gaze as she slipped on the shoes.

If not for the phone call, they would have made love. She felt certain it would have been wonderful. And she *had* wanted it. But ... what then?

Even if she and Kyle had the most romantic weekend on earth, he'd have to return to Seattle on Monday. How often would she see him after that? For a day or two every other week at the beginning, if they were lucky? After that, only once a month?

How long would that go on before they both realized it wasn't working, or he met someone else who lived closer to home? She didn't want to think about the wretched loneliness of those long months of forced separation from Steve.

No. No. She couldn't do that to herself again.

Reluctantly, she said, "I think it'd be best if you went back to the hotel."

"What? Are you serious?"

"Yes."

"You're going to kick me out now, after this?" He gestured toward the bed beneath him.

"You have a hotel room in L.A., don't you?"

"Not anymore. I checked out this morning and moved to a hotel a few miles from here." He stood up and tucked his shirt into his pants. "But I was hoping I wouldn't need it."

She stared at him, dismayed consternation prickling through her. "You were hoping you wouldn't need it? So, you planned to stay here?"

"No. I—"

"Is that what the roses and dinner and show were all about?" she interjected. "A perfectly-planned seduction? Do you play this game on all your business trips? Pick up a woman and see how long it'll take to get her to go to bed with you?"

As soon as the words left her mouth, Desiree regretted them. She wasn't sure why she'd said them. Was she trying to make him angry? In all fairness, she knew that she was as much to blame for what had happened between them as he was. She'd invited him in, had responded to his caresses, had urged him on even when he'd offered to stop.

But she was thinking more clearly now. Now, if she explained everything about her past, would he understand her feelings? She doubted it.

She could see a muscle twitch in his jaw.

"Desiree, I don't make a game of seducing women, on

business trips or anywhere else. I took you out the past few nights because I wanted to be with you. It's that simple."

"And I wanted to be with you," she admitted. "But Kyle … that phone call was a wake-up call. It stopped me from doing something I think I'll regret." Avoiding his eyes, she swallowed hard and added quietly, "What happened just now was … a mistake."

"It was no mistake, and you know it." He looked at her. "This afternoon you were only too willing to let me hold you and kiss you. Just now, you responded to me like a woman on fire—you fanned every spark."

She opened her mouth to protest, then closed it again. Every word he said was true.

He stood up, shoved his hands in his pockets. "When I first heard you on the air, I thought you had a cute radio act with your sultry voice and all those sexual innuendos. But the *real* you, I've discovered, goes way beyond that. Deep down, I think you're a warm, caring person, capable of honest emotions. It's too bad you won't allow yourself to feel them."

He moved to the doorway and fixed her with a look that was equal parts sadness and frustration. "I'm sorry it ended this way, Desiree. I wish you all the best."

His parting footsteps sounded against the hall floor. Her stomach lurched as she heard the door slam with ominous finality.

Then she buried her face in her hands and began to sob.

DESIREE STARED at the mug of coffee in her hands, her thoughts in disarray. Why, oh why, had she said those things to Kyle last night?

She felt horrible about what had happened between them. The expression on his face as he'd left, so filled with aching regret, speared her heart like a knife and echoed her own feelings.

If only she could take those words back. If only she could go back to the way things were before that phone call from the radio station, when they had been in each other's arms, on the verge of making love. If only she hadn't answered the phone!

Absently, she took a sip of coffee, then grimaced. It had gone cold. With a deep sigh, she replaced the mug on the kitchen table, her attention drawn to the arrangement of long-stemmed roses next to the open kitchen window.

Sunlight sparkled like diamonds on the tall, cut-glass vase and burnished the perfect red buds to a velvety sheen. The sight just served to remind her of Kyle's thoughtfulness, his romantic nature.

How often did a man like Kyle come into her life?

Basically, never.

In the few short days that she had known him, he had made her feel pretty and desirable. He had treated her like a queen.

What was it he had said about her last night?

You're a warm, caring person, capable of honest emotions.

And then had come the kicker.

It's too bad you won't allow yourself to feel them.

Tears sprang into her eyes. He was right. From the moment they'd met, she had put up a wall, struggling to deny her attraction to him, knowing that if she allowed herself to get too involved with him, she would just end up getting hurt.

Well, she had gotten hurt—but in a different way than she'd expected. She was hurting not so much because their relationship was over, but because she hadn't even given it a chance.

He was gone. She had ruined everything. And she had no one but herself to blame.

Desiree rose listlessly from the table and had just dumped the cold coffee down the sink, when the now familiar sound of the Maserati engine pulling into the driveway broke the stillness.

What? He was here?

Her stomach knotted. She had no illusions about why he'd come. His jacket and tie were still draped over the chair in her living room. He had only returned to retrieve them.

Would he be businesslike? Cold and aloof? Or charming to the last? There was no way of knowing. Still, she was glad that he'd come back. It would give her a chance to apologize and say a proper goodbye.

When she heard his knock, Desiree crossed the living room and unlocked the front door, trying to figure out what to say, and bracing herself for whatever mood he might be in.

On seeing him, her thoughts evaporated, and her heart went into a skid.

In no way did he resemble a spurned lover who had simply come to retrieve lost property. In his present, casual state of dress he looked more like an athlete on the way to the tennis courts or the gym, and his expression as their eyes collided was both tentative and affectionate.

"Hi," he said softly.

"Hi." The raspy, high-pitched response didn't sound like her own voice. She couldn't help but stare at him, transfixed, one hand glued to the doorknob.

He wore a blue polo shirt, open at the neck. The short sleeves stretched over his well-formed biceps. His legs, long and lean beneath crisp white shorts, were braided with flexible-looking muscles and covered with the same curly dark hair that graced his arms and chest. In one hand he carried a small, white paper bag.

"I'm glad you're up," he said. "I was afraid I'd wake you."

"Oh ... no. I didn't have to work too late. John arrived about half past two."

"Good. So, you got some sleep?"

"Not much." She noticed dark circles under his eyes and wondered if she had them, too.

Her pounding pulse told her how glad she was to see him. Suddenly, in her mind, they were no longer standing like statues in the doorway. They were back in each other's arms last night and he was saying, "You know how I feel about you ... We can never be certain what the future holds for us. But don't let that stop you from living, from loving."

She'd wanted him then. She still did. And she didn't want to waste another minute without telling him so.

"Kyle," Desiree blurted, "I'm so sorry about last night. I didn't mean what I said about us being a mistake. I was just ... scared, I guess."

Relief flooded his features. "I'm sorry, too, if I made you feel bad in any way. Things have been moving at light speed between us. You have every right to feel … whatever and however you feel. And you don't have to make excuses for it."

She swallowed hard, grateful that he was so understanding and magnanimous. "Thanks." Glancing at the paper bag he was holding, she asked, "What's that?"

"Breakfast."

He followed her to the kitchen, where they engaged in small talk at the tiny table as they sipped the freshly brewed coffee she'd made and ate the hot, buttery croissants he'd brought.

When he'd drained his cup, Kyle sat back in his chair and gave her a smile. "So. Do you have any plans for today?"

"Not really."

"I'm glad. Because I've got a surprise for you."

"A surprise?"

"I'm going to take you for a ride in the sky."

A stab of alarm pierced through her. "What do you mean?"

"I rented a plane from the Long Beach Pilots' Club." He grinned like a kid who'd just gotten out of school for the summer. "I'm taking you to Catalina Island for the day."

CHAPTER 7

"Catalina Island?" Desiree's eyes widened in dismay. She'd almost forgotten that Kyle had a pilot's license, that he liked to fly. "You're kidding, right?"

"Why would I be kidding?"

"Because I told you, I don't like to fly. Commercial flights are one thing, but I won't go up in a small plane."

"Desiree: you'll love it. I promise." He leaned forward, his elbows on the table, his face eager with excitement. "It's a thrill you can't even imagine until you've experienced it."

"Maybe for you. But not for me."

"You'll never know if you don't give it a chance."

"I don't want to fly to Catalina. I've read about the airport there. It's dangerous. It's on a high, remote hilltop with a precipitous drop-off. They have a lot of accidents."

"Don't exaggerate. They have more accidents on L.A. freeways in one day than Catalina Airport sees in thirty years. Airplane crashes just make the front pages, that's all."

"Maybe. But still. I read that some pilots compare the Catalina Airport to landing on an aircraft carrier." She shuddered. "Too risky for my blood."

"Everything we do involves a risk of some kind," he returned softly. "What's the point in living if you never venture out into new territory, never take any chances? You might as well be dead."

She took a sharp breath but didn't reply.

"There's nothing to worry about." He gestured with an open palm. "I've been flying for over a decade. I know what I'm doing. The weather is perfect today. And I've made this flight before."

"I'm sorry. If you want to go to Catalina, that's fine, but let's take a boat. I don't want to fly."

He heaved a sigh, struggling visibly to keep his patience. "The cruises to Catalina are all sold out today—I already checked. Even if they weren't, it would have taken hours to get there by boat. We can fly there in fifteen minutes. I've been on the phone since six this morning setting this thing up. I had to pull a few strings to get the plane I wanted. I understand your concerns, and I know this is very short notice, but I made special arrangements on the island. I've got a whole day planned for us. I know you'll love it. I don't want to cancel it all now."

She stood and took a few steps away. "I'm sorry you went to so much trouble. If you were going to make all these elaborate arrangements, you should have asked me first."

He took a deep breath, then let it out slowly. "Okay, you're right. Maybe I should have. I'm sorry if I jumped the gun. But the way things went between us last night, I wanted to arrive with this in my back pocket. This was supposed to be a peace offering. And a surprise."

"I appreciate that," she said slowly, and with utter sincerity, "and the thought behind it. I really do. But it doesn't change the way I feel about flying."

"What's going on, Desiree? Why are you so afraid to fly?"

She let go a long breath. "Because my best friend and her husband were killed in a small plane crash. And I almost went with them that day."

They stared at each other in silence across the table, his face frozen in shock.

After a moment, Desiree went on: "It was just the two of them. Her husband was the pilot. They'd only been married a few months. They were both only twenty-five."

A flicker of anguish shone in his eyes. "I'm so sorry."

"Pam was like a sister to me. And her husband was such a great guy."

"Do they know what caused the accident?"

"They blamed it on the weather. It was foggy, and he was flying too low. They hit a mountain." Her voice cracked, and she cleared her throat before continuing. "When I find myself feeling angry over what happened, when I think what a waste it was that they died so young, at the same time I know how relieved I am that I didn't go with them. And that makes me feel guilty as hell."

He stood up and, in a few quick strides, circled the table and took her in his arms. "I'm sorry, Desiree. So sorry. I wish I could take away the pain you must feel."

With a wavering breath, her arms wrapped around his back. The tears that welled up weren't just tears of sorrow for her dearly missed friends, but tears of relief over being back in Kyle's arms again.

He gave her a quick squeeze, then released her. As he stepped away, an irrational sense of disappointment flooded her at the brevity of his embrace.

"Forget about Catalina," he said. "I'll call and cancel my plans for today. Tell me what *you'd* like to do instead."

THE LARGE WHITE bird stood at attention on the parking strip, wings spread high and wide. Turquoise racing stripes were splashed across the body, nose, and tail, and sunlight gleamed off the wings. A friendly looking plane, Desiree decided, trying hard to ignore the tense knot of anxiety in her stomach. *Maybe this won't be so bad after all ....*

Kyle had been perfectly willing to scrap all his plans. But after all the trouble he'd gone to in arranging this, she'd felt bad turning him down. She'd decided he was right: what *was* the point in living, if you never ventured out into new territory, never took any chances?

Flying was generally safe, she knew that. The weather was perfect—not a speck of fog. And as long as she'd agreed to do it, she was determined to show him what a good sport she could be.

He'd spent a good half hour going over the safety statistics at the Catalina Airport, reassuring her that the plane was practically new, and that he had all the experience required to land there safely.

She leaned against the corrugated aluminum building housing the Long Beach Pilots' Club and watched as Kyle checked over the plane, inside and out, in minute detail.

There was certainly nothing glamorous about private flying. Unlike the sleek sophistication of a modem commercial airport, the Pilots' Club consisted of one small, stark office and a plane-filled parking lot of cracked asphalt, surrounded by a chain-link fence.

She had to admit, though, the idea of hopping into one of these small crafts and simply taking off into the air, the way she might take off down the street in her car, suddenly filled her more with excitement and anticipation than trepidation.

Kyle attached a small metal tow bar to the front of their plane and signaled her to join him. "We need to tow her out of the lot. Grab hold of the wing, would you, and pull?"

Not wanting to show her surprise, Desiree stepped nimbly up to the front of one wing and grabbed the edge with both hands. The rounded ridge of aluminum felt smooth and cool. As Kyle yanked on the tow bar, she gave a mighty tug. To her astonishment the plane rolled forward almost effortlessly.

"Okay, you can let go now," Kyle called. "Just keep an eye on the wing tips. Make sure we're clear of the other planes."

No wonder they call it a light plane, she thought as she watched Kyle tow the plane just past the parking area, her stomach re-knotting with apprehension. The thing seemed as flimsy as a child's toy.

"Let's go!" Kyle called a few minutes later.

She ducked down under the wing as he opened the

cockpit door. "Are you sure this tin can will make it all the way to Catalina?" she asked, striving for a light tone.

"Trust me."

She smiled stiffly as she climbed up onto the smooth, leather seat and he slammed the door. Settling back in her seat, she fastened her safety belt.

Myriad gauges and switches, vaguely reminiscent of her console at the studio, covered the black panel before them. The cockpit was tiny, even smaller than the front section of a foreign compact car.

Well, at least they'd be nice and cozy.

"Do you always do such a thorough check before you take off?" she asked when he'd climbed on board.

"You bet. I'm not taking somebody else's word that this baby's fueled up and in flying condition. I want to see it with my own eyes." He consulted a small handbook on his lap, flipped several switches, and leaned out his open window. "Clear!"

A man working on a nearby plane stepped back and waved. Kyle kicked over the starter and the engine sputtered to life. A voice on the radio began to spew out information like a moderator at an auction. She only caught a few intelligible numbers and phrases.

Kyle picked up the hand microphone. "Long Beach Ground, Cessna nine three six five Uniform, Long Beach Pilots. Taxi to two five left with information Echo."

After a moment's pause the voice on the radio replied with instructions in the same peculiar language. Kyle hung up the mike and grinned. "Funny. Somehow I feel like you should be talking on this thing."

She laughed, finding his relaxed manner a balm to her apprehension. "No way. You talk a different language than any deejay I ever heard. What did they just tell you?"

"The first part was recorded weather information," he said as they taxied toward the runway. "Winds, temperature, altimeter setting. After I identified myself, Ground Control gave me the takeoff point."

"Sounded like Greek to me."

"It's a phonetic alphabet. Helps distinguish one letter from another. Prevents misunderstandings. A is Alpha. B is Bravo. C is Charlie—"

"E is Echo and U is Uniform," she finished for him in comprehension.

"Exactly." He guided the plane onto the runway and pulled to a halt.

As the engine hum increased to a fevered pitch, she stole a glance at Kyle. His mouth curved into a youthful grin and his eyes smoldered with growing excitement, an enthusiasm that was both pleasing to see and contagious.

He called the tower. Her palms began to sweat, and her heart drummed with anticipation. It's going to be okay, she reminded herself. Don't think about what happened to Pam and Tim. It was a freak accident. Kyle knows what he's doing.

A radio voice cleared them for takeoff. "Okay, here we go," Kyle said.

The plane moved forward slowly, then began to pick up speed. The cockpit vibrated. The hum became a roaring buzz in her ears. Vast open fields raced by on both sides. The tower shot past.

The tension in Desiree's stomach heightened. Beads of sweat popped out on her brow. Then, suddenly, her stomach dropped as the plane lifted gracefully off the ground. They were airborne.

"Yee-haw!" Kyle shouted with childlike glee.

"Wow!" Desiree heard herself shout. The anxiety that had built up inside her released itself in a roar of relieved laughter. The plane was buffeted slightly up and down, and the engine continued its loud hum.

Mingled with her fear, she felt an unexpected sense of lighthearted giddiness, as if she'd discovered a newfound sense of freedom.

"That wasn't so bad, was it?" he asked.

She turned to look out her side window. The plane's high wings allowed an undisturbed view of the ground. Familiar streets and landmarks flashed by, and all at once she felt a sense of smug superiority, floating so freely above all the people and cars stuck on the ground.

"This is great," she answered, much to her surprise. "It's almost like a ride at Disneyland."

He laughed with delight and gave her thigh an affectionate squeeze.

In what seemed like minutes they were over the ocean. The dark-blue water shimmered below them. "It's beautiful, Kyle."

He grinned, his hands on the controls. "I knew you'd like it."

When they reached the island, Kyle circled slowly around it and she held her breath in wonder.

No Mediterranean island could be more beautiful than

the sight of Santa Catalina as it rose majestically out of the sea. All dark browns and greens against the crystal blue ocean, the island's jagged shoreline was interrupted by only a few small harbors and scattered beaches.

After Kyle received his landing instructions, Desiree eyed the island's mountainous interior with concern. They swept past the island, over the ocean, then circled around the back again. "Where's the airport?" she asked.

"Right there." He pointed toward a high mountain plateau bisected by a ribbon of asphalt.

"That's the runway?"

"Yes."

Her mouth went dry. Even the reports she'd read hadn't prepared her for the sight of something quite so scary. The short, paved road began just beyond a sharp drop-off.

And ended at the edge of another cliff dropping straight down to the sea.

The cliff loomed closer. The engine roar quieted to a low hum. The plane slowed, aiming straight for the cliff's top edge.

"I can't look!" Desiree cried, leaning her head back against the seat and closing her eyes.

"Nothing to worry about," he said reassuringly. "I've done this before. We're fine."

She nodded mutely. *Nothing to worry about. We're fine.* She chanted the words over and over to herself.

Suddenly she felt a lifting sensation, as if they'd floated up on a strong breeze. Then the plane drifted downward and touched ground more smoothly than she could have ever imagined.

Desiree could almost feel the brakes grabbing as the plane quickly decelerated, the vibration traveling through her body with blinding force. Her heart pounded violently as they slowed to a taxiing speed, then expertly turned and rolled on.

She opened her eyes and took a deep breath, noting that he had landed quite a distance away from the drop-off at the other end of the cliff.

"Nothing to it, was there?" he grinned.

She smiled, relief surging through her, along with a sense of admiration for his piloting skills. "Piece of cake."

"EVERYTHING'S HERE, just the way I wanted it." Kyle tossed the beach bag they'd brought into the trunk of the waiting sedan.

"What have you got in there?" Desiree glanced curiously toward the back of the car, but he shut the trunk with a clang.

"You'll see."

He opened the door for her, and she slid into the bucket seat. At his direction, she'd put on her bathing suit under her shorts and T-shirt in the airport rest room. He now wore sleek navy-blue bathing trunks, and a denim shirt hung loosely over his white T-shirt.

"How did you manage to get this car?" she asked after he'd climbed in and shut the door. "I heard that they don't rent cars on the island."

His eyes glittered mysteriously. "They don't."

"You must know someone who lives here, then."

"I do." He started the engine and headed out of the airport lot.

Noting the direction he was taking, she said, "This isn't the road to Avalon, is it?"

She'd taken a one-day cruise to Catalina two years before and had spent the afternoon with hordes of other sightseers, combing through the shops and museum in Avalon, the island's one and only small harbor town.

"No. I can only take so much of that touristy stuff."

"So where are we going?"

"You'll see," he said again. "I have something completely different in mind for us today."

The narrow, winding road hugged the dry, desolate mountain on one side and dropped off sharply on the other. The terrain resembled a desert wilderness, mostly scrub oak, rock, and cacti.

Soon, they rounded a bend and she caught sight of a small, lonely stretch of sand below rocky cliffs. He turned onto a bluff above the beach and parked. There wasn't another car or human being in sight.

"Oh, Kyle, how wonderful."

She jumped out of the car and ran to the edge of the bluff. A winding path along the cliffs led to a deserted beach below. She gazed down with growing excitement at the sparkling white sand and the gently rolling surf beyond. The hot sun blazed in a cloudless sky over an endless, shimmering blue sea.

"I've never seen a beach so empty on a Saturday. Why isn't anyone else here?"

Kyle stepped up beside her. "Tourists can't rent cars, so the only people who can get here are the islanders, and there aren't many of those. This is the smallest beach, and the farthest from town, so I figured if we were lucky, we'd have it to ourselves." He raised an inquiring eyebrow in her direction. "Like it?"

"It's incredible. It's like being shipwrecked on a desert island. It's paradise."

He turned to face her. "I hoped you'd feel this way. I was here once on my own, several years ago. I've always dreamed of coming back, when I had someone special to share it with."

Yesterday, she thought, he'd have wrapped his arms around her waist and whispered those words against her ear. She glanced up wistfully at him. After the things she'd said last night, he was probably afraid she'd shrink back again if he got too close—and she couldn't blame him.

"I'm glad I'm the special someone you chose," Desiree said softly.

She could tell he was pleased by the soft glow in his green eyes. "So am I," he answered.

"Now *here's* what I call an ideal picnic spot." Kyle set down the ice chest and wicker basket next to the rocky cliff and pulled out a folded blanket from the beach bag.

Desiree helped him spread the large, soft blanket across the sand, then paused to admire the spot they'd found. The hot sun baked the beach like a giant oven.

But this little, sandy alcove at the far end of the beach dipped in under the shade of dark, overhanging rocks, hiding them from view of the bluff high above. Just a dozen yards away the surf lapped the shore, but here the sand was fine and soft.

"I can't wait to try the water," she said.

"Me too. But how about if we eat first? I'm starving."

Kyle peeled off his denim shirt and T-shirt. She couldn't resist a glance at the broad expanse of his smooth back as he raised his arms over his head, and the taut muscles of his abdomen when he turned to face her. She had to restrain the urge to close the gap between them and curl her arms about his slim waist.

To distract herself, she dropped down on the blanket and eyed the picnic basket. "Sounds great. What have you got in here?"

"Just a few odds and ends." He knelt and opened the lid of the picnic basket, then proceeded to lift out its contents: a small French bread, knives, a wooden cutting board, napkins, plates, and utensils.

From the cooler he produced three kinds of cheese, a salami, a tin of pâté de fois gras, green grapes, apples, a jar of black olives, and a relish tray. Finally he pulled out a frosty bottle of champagne and two stemmed glasses.

"Where did you get all this?" she asked in amazement.

"I told you I was up at six this morning making phone calls." Smiling, he expertly opened the bottle and filled her chilled glass with the sparkling wine. "The owner of the Avalon Grand Hotel is a friend of mine. He had the restaurant put this together for us. Oh, and one more thing." He reached back in the cooler and lifted up a six-pack of Sparkle Light soda. "In case you're still thirsty after the champagne."

She laughed in delight. "Lucky me, to know someone with such terrific connections."

When he'd filled his own glass, he raised it to hers in a toast. "To four unforgettable days, and many more just like them."

Desiree felt a little pang at that—this hopeful mention of the future—but tried to tell herself that anything was possible. She clinked her glass lightly against his with a facetious smile. "To the best pilot to whom I've ever entrusted my life."

She took a sip of the crisp, tangy wine and sighed in satisfaction as she felt the refreshing coolness revitalize her system. They feasted on the assortment of delicacies as they enjoyed the cool shade under the overhanging cliff, the sound of the rolling waves, and the pleasant, fresh scent of the sea air.

After they packed up the leftovers, Kyle dipped back into the cooler, brought out two small, covered bowls, and handed one to Desiree with a flourish.

"*Ta da! La piece de resistance.*"

"Chocolate mousse!" Desiree cried. "Another one of my favorites. How did you know?"

"A lucky guess. It's one of my favorites, too."

Desiree picked up a spoon and dove in. A mesmerized smile crossed her face as she savored the cold, creamy chocolate. "Mmm, this is heaven. I've been *dying* for chocolate the past two days."

He scooted next to her and slipped one hand around her to rest on her waist. "A bona fide chocaholic, huh?"

"In the worst possible way."

She felt herself tremble under the touch of his fingers,

and briefly closed her eyes. *Desiree,* he'd said last night, *you take my breath away.*

To her disappointment—as if afraid he was getting too close—Kyle abruptly withdrew his hand and reached for the champagne bottle. "Shall we finish this off?"

All night I've been dying to hold you ... kiss you ... touch you like this. She swallowed over the lump in her throat. "You bet."

He emptied the bottle into their glasses. They sat side by side on the blanket, finished their desert, and sipped the bubbly wine. Desiree glanced at his bare thigh, so close to her own, recalling his words from the night before.

There's nothing more beautiful than what we feel for each other right now, he'd told her. *I don't want to hurt you, my darling. I only want to love you.*

The thought that followed came unbidden, yet she realized, with a start, it had been smoldering at the edge of her consciousness, just waiting for her to acknowledge it.

In the short time they'd been together, she'd come to feel closer to Kyle than to anyone she'd ever known. Despite the brevity of their relationship and all her reservations about the future, she was, just as she'd feared, falling in love with him.

Somehow though, to her surprise, the realization made her feel happy instead of worried or scared.

"Penny for your thoughts."

Her head whipped up. "What?" *Could she tell him? No—of course not.* "Oh, I was just thinking ... how beautiful it is here. And how much I've enjoyed everything."

He drained his glass and set it back in the basket. "Even the flight?"

"Even the flight," she admitted. "It was a thrill. The biggest thrill I've ever experienced."

"*The* biggest thrill?" His voice had a teasing lilt to it.

She blushed. "Yeah. I know—how lame am I? But it's true. It was *the* biggest thrill."

He smiled. "I'm glad. Now what do you say we go jump in that water?"

"All right." She shook her head to clear it, then pushed herself to a stand. As she shrugged quickly out of her top and shorts, she heard his soft whistle.

"Nice bathing suit." His eyes slid down her body, pausing at the rise of her breasts above the skimpy royal blue bikini top and then lingering along the curves of her waist, hips, and legs.

"Thank you."

He cleared his throat and grinned devilishly. "But the truth is, you don't really need it. We're the only people here. There's no path at this end of the beach. And the only creatures who are likely to happen by from the ocean side are the feathered variety."

"I'm not going to skinny dip," she insisted with a laugh.

"Suit yourself. Let's do this."

He grabbed her hand and pulled her with him into the sparkling waves. She gasped as the cold water splashed against her calves and then enveloped her to the waist.

She would have preferred to proceed more slowly, to take a few minutes to adjust to the water, but in typical Kyle fashion he plunged ahead, urging her forward along with him.

Were the sudden shivers traveling up her spine due to the brisk water temperature, or to the splendid sight of the half-naked, virile man beside her, and the feeling of his hand in hers? She couldn't be sure.

Finally, he let go of her hand and dove forward under a wave. He emerged a few feet beyond, spraying water and laughing. "Want to swim out a ways?"

"Yes." A strong swimmer, Desiree happily knifed forward through the water. Her body gradually adjusted to the temperature, which now felt delightfully invigorating.

They swam side by side for a time, rising up to crest each gentle wave, and then turned to ride the tide back in. When he reached a spot where he could touch bottom, he stopped and pulled her into his arms.

"Fantastic, isn't it?"

In answer she wrapped her arms around his neck, laughing and nodding. Suddenly their eyes met, and she felt his entire body stiffen, as if struggling to keep his emotions in check. Desiree's heart beat a jagged rhythm as they bobbed up and down together with the waves.

His eyes seemed to echo his words of last night. *You know how I feel about you. I've made no secret of it. Do you feel the same way about me?*

Yes! her mind cried. *Yes*. Can't you see? I adore you!

He brought one hand up to the nape of her neck and kissed her lightly. With a small moan she parted his lips with her tongue and deepened the kiss, sighing with pleasure as he wrapped his tongue around hers.

A lightning bolt of desire flashed through her body, touching each vital organ, the tips of her breasts, the center of her womanhood.

His arms tightened around her as he kissed her slowly, lovingly. He brought up one hand to cover her breast, kneading it gently beneath his caressing fingers. The ocean lapped and rolled against them, a frenzied counterpoint to their mounting passion.

"You're lovely, Desiree. Every perfect inch of you."

He fused his mouth to hers once more and she lifted her legs to clasp around his waist. She recalled the words he'd spoken the first time they walked on a beach, just one day after they met:

You are Desiree ... Desired. Wanted. Longed for.

A shiver passed through her body as she felt his manhood, hard with desire, press against the cove of her femininity. They might as well have been naked, for all the protection that their thin bathing suits provided between them.

Let me show you how much I care. Let me make love to you, he'd said last night. With sudden force he freed her mouth, and she felt rather than heard his passionate groan.

"Desiree," he whispered thickly. "I told you we'd wait until you were ready—and we will. But can you feel how much I want you?"

"Yes." *And I want you.* The acknowledgement came from deep in her soul and she wrapped her arms more tightly around him, as if by holding him close he could never leave her side.

What's the point in living if you never take risks? They lived separate lives, could probably share no more than an instant in time together. But somehow it didn't matter anymore.

She'd spent far too long, she realized, avoiding the possibility of pain. All she had to show for it was years of loneliness.

She knew what was to come would be sweet and precious, a treasure to look back on all the years of her life. They were meant for each other now; this moment was as inevitable as the ebb and flow of the swirling tide.

Her voice was a soft plea against his ear. "Make love to me."

CHAPTER 8

She was glad that he didn't hesitate. He carried her out of the water and across the sand, laid her down on the soft wide blanket in the shelter of the cliff, and stretched out beside her.

He held her for a long moment before he kissed her, his hands combing through the wet hair streaming across her shoulders.

She relished the feel of his cool, wet body against hers, drank in his clean scent, and savored the salty taste of his skin beneath her lips. She felt her heart drumming riotously beneath her breast and knew he must feel it, too.

When he bent his head to kiss her, his lips moved softly, earnestly, slowly over hers. Each light touch of his mouth was like a mind-stealing drug, warming and soothing her already willing body and brain.

As she returned his kiss, her hands massaged the smooth, firm muscles of his slippery wet back, which flexed with each movement of his arms and body against hers.

He ran his fingers the length of her slender back to the edge of her bikini bottoms, then up again, to the ties holding her top. With a single tug he untied the bow at her back.

He kissed her once more leisurely, as if to savor each tiny moment and heighten their pleasure by prolonging the anticipation. At last, he drew back and lifted the wisp of fabric over her head.

He gently rolled her to her back, swept his fingers over her bare breasts and down the curves of her waist, then nimbly removed her bikini bottoms.

She marveled over her lack of embarrassment. Never in her life had she felt such pride in her body. A thrill raced through her under Kyle's impassioned gaze.

"You're a goddess," he whispered, eyes shining with tenderness and delight. After slipping off his bathing trunks, with loving fingers, he traced the inside of her thighs.

"You're so beautiful," she replied in kind. "All day I've wanted to touch you, hold you."

A smile twitched his lips as he lay suddenly still beside her, propped on one elbow. "Please. Feel free."

Hesitantly, she ran her fingers through the soft hair that covered his upper chest, then sifted down through the satiny trail toward the dimple of his navel and his hardened masculinity. She felt his stomach contract and heard his rapid intake of breath.

A sudden sound startled them both. They turned to find that a seagull had dropped to the sand a few yards away. Then, just as quickly as it had come, the bird spread its wings and darted away across the waves.

They shared a soft laugh. Kyle grasped her hand in his, turned it against his lips and kissed each one of her knuckles in turn. "Are you okay?" he asked softly. "Does it feel strange to be here with me, like this, on the beach?"

Did it feel strange?

No, she thought. *It feels right. Oh, so right.* His entire body spoke of his longing for her, and the fire burning within her told her how much she wanted him.

The overhanging rocks sheltered them from view above, and the distant rolling surf played a melodious symphony beneath the canopy of the bright blue sky. It was as if this secluded, shaded alcove was meant for them alone.

"Do you want to stop?" His low voice was concerned.

A rush of affection welled in her throat. Twice now she'd told him to stop, asked him to leave when his desire for her was all too evident. Still, he was willing to call it off now if she was uncertain. She'd never met anyone so understanding or unselfish.

His eyes as they met hers were filled with a yearning that surpassed sexual desire. He wanted her. But not just her body. She knew he cared about her, that he was sensitive to her needs, her feelings. Her heart went out to him wholly.

"I don't want to stop," she whispered. "It's just been a long time. I think I'm a little nervous."

"Don't be. Relax. Enjoy the pleasure we can give each other."

Their mouths touched tentatively at first, as his fingers paid loving attention to one of her breasts. Her hands moved caressingly up and down his sides, acquainting themselves with the lean hardness of his hips and hair-roughened thighs.

Then their lips began to move faster, faster. Tongues delved, tasted, explored, driven by hunger and the need to fulfill their long-restrained passion.

Her hands roved down his back, cupped his firm buttocks and pulled him more tightly against her. She felt his urgent desire between them. He groaned low and deep in his chest as he kissed the corners of her lips, her cheeks, the length of her throat.

Their breath came in quick gasps now as their hands moved over each other without restraint, each caress becoming bolder, more intimate. His nibbling teeth against her sensitive neck brought every cell in her body to full jolting awareness.

His mouth moved with seductive slowness across her shoulders and over the curves of her breasts. She wound her fingers through his damp hair as his palm prowled across her ribcage and abdomen, then lower, and lower still.

And then he was there. Questing fingers gently parted her thighs, sought, and found. Tremors shot through her as he probed the pulsing source of her passion, mesmerizing her with their gentle accuracy.

She writhed beneath him, a molten core of need, mindless to everything but the tributes his hands and lips were paying to her body.

I want you, I want you, her body sang. *Now! Now!*

With an impassioned groan, she curled her fingers around his hard biceps, pulling him up on top of her. There was no need to speak. Their eyes locked, communicating their mutual hunger more eloquently than words.

With trembling fingers, she guided him into the inviting silk of her body. She felt a sensation of piercing tightness, an injection of smooth liquid fire that blended with the flames raging within her, and she whimpered with joy and relief.

"Does it hurt?" he whispered against her lips, his eyes filled as much with passion as compassion. "Tell me."

"A bit. But that's okay." It was a welcome pain, and she knew it wouldn't last long. His body molded perfectly to hers, like two missing pieces of a puzzle finally joined.

The hurt gave way to a sweet, violent throbbing as she matched his rhythmic movements with her own. She heard the call of a gull again, and the lulling sound of the waves seemed to surround her.

She opened her eyes for an instant to glimpse the brilliant blue sky, then shut them again, nearly bursting with the joy of sharing this moment with him in this beautiful, magical place.

Did it ever feel like this before? she wondered. Ever?

Her body tensed with anticipation and impending need. For an instant she froze, suspended in time, and then in a burst of light she broke free, her inner core pulsing with climactic shudders, which carried her high into the air.

Moments later she heard his soft moans as he lost himself in his own release. She wrapped herself around him, her mind floating freely, her body reveling in his closeness and warmth. Then ever so slowly, they drifted together back to earth.

Many minutes passed as they held each other and regained their breath. She opened her eyes and smiled into his. The corners of his mouth lifted up in a grin.

He rolled them gently to their sides, bodies still clinging together, arms and legs entwined, tips of noses touching. She caressed his cheek lovingly with her palm, trying to memorize the texture of his skin, the exact slope of his nose, the angles of his cheek and jaw.

"I take it back, Kyle," she said at last, a teasing gleam in her eyes.

"Hmmm?"

"The plane ride today was only the *second* most thrilling experience of my life."

She felt her grin start just as his shoulders began to shake. Then, eyes shining, they both laughed out loud.

DESIREE AWOKE AND STRETCHED LAZILY. Memories of the night before filtered into her mind, filling her with a sense of complete contentment.

A sleepy smile curved her lips as her eyes snapped open. To her dismay, the pillow beside her was empty. A sudden ache swept over her. Where was he?

A low, cheerful whistle and the smell of freshly brewed coffee drifted in from the kitchen. With a happy, relieved sigh, she relaxed beneath the covers and closed her eyes again.

It was a night she'd never forget. Just thinking about it made her pulse race with pleasure. They had returned from the island just before dark, still glowing from their passionate encounter on the beach.

"I could make love to you all night long, and it still wouldn't be enough," Kyle said later, after they'd taken a long, luxurious shower together.

She'd smiled alluringly. "Try me."

And so he did. They made love again and again, and each time was better than the last. He carried her to heights of ecstasy she'd never imagined were possible, all the while treating her with infinite tenderness and affection.

Sometimes, afterwards, they'd looked into each other's eyes and laughed, just as they had that afternoon, overwhelmed by the sense of pure joy that enveloped them.

Other times they slept, enveloped in the warm cocoon of each other's arms, only to awaken in the moonlit darkness more filled with desire than before.

"How was I lucky enough to find you?" he'd said as he cradled her against his chest.

"I've never known anyone like you, Kyle. It's never been like this for me before."

"For me either. My lovely Desiree ...."

Never in her life had she felt so cherished, so adored. He awakened desires within her she'd never believed existed.

"Touch me," he'd said. "There. Ahh, that's it. If you only knew how good that feels ...."

Her marriage bed, she saw now, had been functional and routine compared to the loving she shared with Kyle. It seemed there was no part of her body left untouched by the warm pressure of his lips, the magic of his fingers.

"Your skin is so soft. So smooth. So feminine. I love the way it feels here. And here."

"And you're so hard. Everywhere. Especially ... here."

He had chuckled softly. "Do you like ... this?"

"Like it? Oh! Kyle ...."

As she thought back over everything she'd said, every wanton thing she'd done, her cheeks flushed hotly. Was the woman who behaved with such unashamed abandon last night really *her?*

Yes! And she'd loved every second of it.

Desiree threw off the sheet and darted into the bathroom. As she brushed her teeth, she grinned. She couldn't remember when she'd ever so looked forward to a new day. She'd slept very little; she ought to feel exhausted. Instead, she felt completely revitalized. She was so gloriously happy, she felt like she was floating on air.

Hearing footsteps in the hall, she returned to bed and propped herself up against the headboard, watching the doorway where morning sunlight filtered in through the half-open curtains.

He stepped in quietly, wearing only his navy-blue bathing trunks and carrying a black leather garment bag. As she feasted her eyes on each well-sculpted muscle, each detail of the strong, masculine body she'd come to know so well, a shiver of pure delight ran through her.

All at once, it occurred to her that he was standing very still and was staring at her in much the same manner; and she blushed.

"Good morning," he said, his voice so low and rough she barely caught the words.

"Good morning." She glanced down briefly, suddenly

aware of how she must look to him, with her tousled hair framing her face, her amber eyes still flushed with a sleepy-warm glow, and her naked body stretched out in full view. She reached for the sheet to cover herself, but he said:

"Don't."

His tone was soft, flattering, affectionate, disarming. She left the sheet alone.

He took a deep breath as if trying to reassemble his thoughts. Finally, he said: "I hope you don't mind if I hang up a few things. This has been sitting out in the car for two days."

"Please, be my guest." She swung her legs off the bed and crossed the room to him.

He opened her closet, hung his garment bag inside. Unzipping the case, he moved two suits and shirts out onto the closet rod. They looked hopelessly wrinkled.

Her arms encircled his waist. "You can't wear those. We'll have to iron them."

"Don't worry about it. I have every confidence that they'll spring back to life by tomorrow."

"I doubt it."

He drew her closer. "Well, I won't need them for a while, anyway."

"Oh? What were you planning on wearing today?"

"The same thing you're wearing. Nothing."

"Nothing?"

"Absolutely nothing." He kissed her. "Mmmm. You taste minty."

"You taste delicious. Like coffee."

Kissing her again, he heaved a sigh of pleasure, then said, "By the way, I was right."

"About what?"

"We made love all night long, and it still wasn't enough." With an animal-like growl, he picked her up, set her back down on the bed, and leaped on top of her.

"Wait!" she cried. "Kyle! We haven't eaten since lunch yesterday at the beach. I'm famished. I've got to eat something."

He smiled wickedly into her eyes. "I can think of something I'd like to nibble on right now. But ... I'll settle for this." He pretended to take a bite out of her shoulder.

She writhed with laughter beneath him, finally managing to roll away and drop off the side of the bed. Taking a few steps backward, she grabbed her hairbrush from the dresser and brandished it like a weapon, her eyes flashing dangerously.

"Come near me again and I'll strike where you'll most regret it."

He stood up and raised his palms. "Truce! I surrender. We'll take a food break. But first, I have to run."

"Run?"

He nodded. "*Run*. As in jog. You know, that's where you move quickly, one foot after the other, like this." He darted around the bed and grabbed her. Her scream ended abruptly as his mouth came down on hers. He kissed her soundly, then released her again. "Don't you ever run?"

"Yes," she said breathlessly. "Three mornings a week."

"So do I. At least I try to. But it rains so much in Seattle, I can't jog as often as I'd like. I want to make the most of your gorgeous weather while I'm here. Care to join me?"

His reference to his hometown sent a stab of pain piercing through her, reminding her of how short their time together would be. Her smile wavered, but she resurrected it quickly. "I'd love to run with you. Let's put on some clothes."

They did warm-up exercises together on her living-room floor, then jogged through her neighborhood to a nearby park. She kept pace with him easily, enjoying the warm sunshine and the smell of the freshly mown grass.

She gazed frequently at Kyle as they ran, trying to memorize the pleasure of this moment, to push the thought of his leaving out of her mind.

More than once during their lovemaking the night before, she'd wanted to burst out with a heartfelt *I love you, Kyle.*

She knew it now. She wasn't *falling* in love with him. *She loved him.* She felt it in every fiber of her being, knew it as surely as she knew the sun would set that night and rise the next morning. But how could she tell him?

His own whispered endearments had made her feel that she was as special to him as he'd become to her. But he'd never said he loved her—and why would he? They'd only known each other a few short days.

As he'd pointed out, everything had happened at light speed between them. She didn't expect him to fall in love overnight, just because she had. Even so, that didn't make her feelings any less real, or do anything to soften the pain of their impending separation.

Let's just take things one day at a time, he'd said the other night. Were a few days together all he had in mind? After he left on Monday, would she ever see him again? *Of course you will,* she told herself. *Don't be ridiculous.* But when? How often? And for how long?

It suddenly became a Herculean task to draw breath into her lungs as she ran. She wondered if he often spent weekends away from home this way. How many women had enjoyed the delights of his lovemaking, the passionate warmth of his embrace?

Don't think about it, she cautioned herself. *Just enjoy the little time you have.*

After they returned and took a shower, they made breakfast together in her cozy kitchen. Kyle, his bare back magnificent above a pair of white shorts, stood at the stove and cooked a fluffy omelet filled with mushrooms, cheese, and crisply fried ham.

After throwing on a halter top and shorts, Desiree prepared freshly squeezed orange juice and toasted English muffins. They ate at her tiny kitchen table, crowded by the vase of red roses he'd sent three days before.

"Nice flowers," Kyle said as he speared a forkful of omelet. "Where'd you get those? Some love-sick fan?"

"Sick is not the word. The man's a maniac." She grinned at him across the table. "He hasn't let me sleep for the past four nights."

"Four nights?" His eyes narrowed with mock jealousy. "I can vouch for the fact that you didn't get any sleep *last* night. But what happened the three nights before?"

She reached across the table to caress his bare forearm. "Who could sleep after our first date, or after the way you kissed me the next night, when we got home from the beach? And on Friday, after you left …."

"Let's not talk about that. It's past. Forgotten." He seized her hand in both of his and squeezed it. For a long moment he was silent, staring down at their interlocked hands atop the table.

Suddenly he drew back with a frown, tapping his fingertips on the table. "Why do you have this awful table, anyway? What's it made of?"

"Formica."

"Why on earth do you have a Formica kitchen table? Everything else in this house is a beautiful antique."

He had a point. The table was stained, sported burn marks, and was cracked along one edge. Teasingly, she said, "You don't like my 1950s pink Formica? What's wrong with you? It's a classic."

"Pink? What do you mean, pink? The table's white."

"It's pink."

He bent closer, staring at the tabletop. "Really? Pink?"

"Pink. Pale pink."

"It looks white to me." He shrugged, then shook his head. "Good grief, a pink Formica table. And I thought white was bad."

She frowned with feigned indignation. "This table's the height of chic. The epitome of class. Besides, it—"

"—was my great-grandmother's," they finished in unison. He rolled his eyes. She nodded.

"I think it's great that you were named after her," he said, pointing his fork at her. "It's a beautiful name. But you didn't have to take every piece of furniture she had."

She laughed. "It *is* hideous, isn't it?"

"Why don't you get a nice table? Mahogany, to match your living-room set? Your dining room is practically empty."

"I never had any reason to buy another table. I don't

have people over for dinner very often." She finished the last of her coffee and shrugged. "I've had to move so often. This table is sturdy, and I don't have to worry if it gets banged up."

He frowned again. "Does it bother you? Having to move all the time?"

"It comes with the territory. Radio's a part of me I can't give up. Moving is a condition I've had to accept."

"What about now? They seem to love you at KICK. Do you think they'll keep you on indefinitely?"

"There's no such word as *indefinitely* in a radio station's vocabulary." She toyed with her empty coffee cup, finally lifting her eyes to his. "But I'm grateful to be here. I have a terrific job, and good jobs are hard to come by. I'll stay as long as they'll keep me."

He opened his mouth to speak, then seemed to think better of it. All at once he stood, walked around to her side of the table, and gently pulled her to her feet, holding her hands in his.

"What do you love most about being a deejay?"

"Everything."

"Everything?" He lifted one of her hands to his lips and kissed it. "Really?"

Considering, she amended her statement. "Well, admittedly, there *is* a burnout factor. After you've played and talked about the same song two hundred times, it's pretty hard to think up something original to say. Even so, it's …."

"It's what?" He dropped tiny kisses from her palm along the length of her arm, causing exquisite chills to shiver through her.

She was finding it increasingly difficult to think. "It's ... exciting, stimulating."

His lips reached her shoulder as he pulled her closer. When his tongue flicked over the sensitive spot at the side of her throat, she drew a deep, wavering breath.

"Stimulating?" he said softy.

"Yes. I can be beautiful on the air. I can stir people's imaginations."

"You don't need to go on the air for that. You're beautiful in person." He deftly untied her halter top at the nape of her neck and tugged downward. The top dropped and her breasts flexed out to his admiring view.

"You're stimulating," he added, pulling her into his tight embrace. With a gasp she felt the ridge of his masculinity burrow into her abdomen.

"And you definitely stir my imagination," he said as he covered her mouth with his.

"What do you do about clothes?"

"Clothes?"

Darkness had just descended. They'd spent the afternoon in and out of bed. Mostly in. They'd ignored the outside world, as if nothing existed but the two of them and the feelings they shared in this tiny, stolen moment in time.

Since it had been too hot to cook, Desiree had made a chef's salad for dinner, which she'd served with the bottle of Chablis she'd put in the refrigerator that morning.

Now, their appetite sated, they relaxed together in the

redwood swing on her back patio. The cool night air, perfumed with the scent of orange blossoms from the tree in her backyard, felt delightfully refreshing. They'd each donned shorts and a T-shirt, and Desiree wore the songbird pendant Kyle had admired on their first date.

She tipped the last of the ice-cold Chablis into the stemmed glass in Kyle's hand. "If you can't see certain colors, how do you know what clothes go together?"

"I don't. I have to rely on what the salesclerks tell me at the store, buy things as a set, and always wear them that way. I stick to gray, blue, white, and brown most of the time, so that even if I make a mistake about what goes with what, it won't look too horrendous."

She was silent for a moment, savoring the wine's delicate aroma and dry, tangy taste as she pondered his dilemma. "It must be frustrating."

"At times." He grinned. "When I was a kid, my sisters used to laugh at me when I tried to adjust the color on the TV set. They'd mix up the clothes in my drawer, so I wore things that looked ridiculous together. They teased me about it mercilessly at school."

"I was teased at school, too. About the color of my eyes." She told him about the nickname that kids had given her, Stoplight, and how much it hurt even now to think about it.

"I love the color of your eyes. Kids can be so cruel."

"They can."

He sighed. "I still have a lot of trouble with socks, telling the browns from the blacks and blues."

"You need a wife to help you dress." The moment she

said the words she regretted them. What a stupid thing to say!

His eyes opened wide. His eyebrows lifted. He studied her with earnest amusement. "Maybe I do."

She averted her eyes, cleared her throat. "It wasn't very nice, what your sisters did."

"No, but I made up for it. One night when I was a senior in high school, the four oldest girls were sitting around the living room in bathrobes and curlers, with mud masks plastered all over their faces. They were in their teens at the time. I called a bunch of my friends and asked them to come over, guys they all had crushes on."

"Kyle! You didn't."

"I did."

Desiree burst out laughing. "They must have died of embarrassment."

"I was blacklisted for months."

"I guess they deserved it."

"I guess they did."

He sipped his wine, watching his fingertip trail along her shoulder and down her arm. A quiet sadness filled his eyes and his voice as he said suddenly, "I'm going to miss you."

His change of mood caught her off-guard and brought a lump to her throat. She looked away. Why was he bringing it up now? She knew this was their last evening together, but she'd avoided thinking about it, the way one avoids thinking about the inevitable end of a wonderful vacation. You know it'll be over soon, and you'll have to go home. But you put it out of your mind. You don't let it spoil your fun.

"I'll miss you, too," she said softly.

"I wish things were different. I wish I didn't live so far away, that we could—"

"It's okay." Suddenly the wine tasted bitter. She set down her glass next to the swing. "You don't have to explain."

"I do. I want you to know how much this weekend has meant to me. You're a very special woman, Desiree. I care for you a great deal. It's not going to be easy going back, putting myself through the usual routine, knowing you're over a thousand miles away."

She pressed her lips together, not trusting herself to speak.

He drained his glass and set it down. Gently taking her into his arms, he caressed her shoulders and ran his lips over her hair. "I wish I could stay longer, but I can't. I've got an important meeting tomorrow afternoon. I have to leave first thing in the morning."

"I understand. I didn't expect you to stay longer." Her voice cracked and she inhaled a sobbing breath as tears welled up in her eyes.

"Don't cry, sweetheart. Don't cry."

"I'm not." She squeezed her eyes shut, swallowed hard, and willed the threatening tears to dissolve. "I knew we would only have a few days together. I tried so hard, at first, not to get involved with you because I knew it couldn't last. But …."

He pulled back and stared at her. "Who says it can't last?"

"You know it can't. You said at the beginning, 'let's take things one day at a time.' So, I did. But let's be realistic.

Where can it go from here? What kind of future could we build, with you firmly planted in Seattle, and me here?"

"We'll make it work," he said emphatically.

"How? How often could we see each other?"

"Weekends. Every single weekend. Plenty of couples who live in the same town don't see each other more often than that."

"Every weekend? How can we? It'd cost a fortune."

"Who cares? I'll pay for the airline tickets. I'll do all the traveling if you want."

"You can't fly down here every single weekend."

"I can and I will."

She shook her head. "We'll only make each other miserable."

"I expect to be miserable five days a week. But we're going to live gloriously on the weekends."

He slid next to her, stretching one arm behind her along the back of the swing. Lifting the pendant at her throat, he held it up to the moonlight and studied it appreciatively. "Nothing is going to keep me away from my songbird."

"Kyle …."

"By the way," he added, "I may have another excuse to come down here. Often."

"Oh? Why?"

"I flew down originally for a meeting with a potential client. While I was here, I took a look at a manufacturing plant in L.A. I'm considering buying it."

Her pulse quickened. "Really?"

"I expect to make a decision in the next week or two." He took one of her hands in his and squeezed it. "If I do buy the company, I'll be flying down for a week at a time, especially at first while things are getting set up."

A small flame of hope lit up inside her. Could it be true? A week at a time?

Then the flame died down and a voice inside her cried, *What difference would it make? Someday you'd have to leave. Who knows where you'll end up? And you'll be back where you started.*

He cupped her cheek in his hand and caressed her with his gaze. "But no matter what happens, I'll be down here as often as I can to see you. Believe that."

A lone tear trickled down her cheek. "I do. I believe you mean it now." She grasped his hand, pulled it away from her face and held it in her lap. "But I don't see how it can last, Kyle. One of us will get hurt in the end."

He sighed in exasperation. "Desiree, didn't this weekend mean anything to you? Don't you care enough about me to even try to make this work?"

"Yes! I care about you," she cried. "More than any man I've ever met. I wish more than anything that we could be together. I'll be miserable the moment you leave. But a long-distance relationship can't work. It feels … impossible."

"What makes you think it's impossible? Have you ever tried it?"

"Yes."

"When?"

"When I left my husband!"

CHAPTER 9

A tense silence reigned for several moments. Desiree stared straight ahead at the dark stretch of yard beyond the patio light's glow, unwilling to meet his gaze.

"Tell me, Desiree," he said finally, his voice soft and deep. "Tell me what happened."

She leaned her head back against the wooden swing beneath his outstretched arm. She sighed, then spoke in a low monotone.

"I met Steve the first night I arrived in Tucson to start a new job. He was an attorney, very smart, very successful. We hit it off right away, and before I knew it, we were living together. One night, about six months later, we were out having a few drinks, and a friend of Steve's stopped by our table and asked us when we were going to get married. 'What's wrong with right now?' Steve said.

"I don't know when I've ever been so excited. I loved him, I really loved him, and he said that he loved me. He grabbed my hand and we got in his car and drove all the way to Las Vegas. We got married at one of those little chapels at two in the morning ... you know the kind, where a justice of the peace reads a few well-memorized words, and his wife stands by in her bathrobe, smiling and yawning and wishing you luck."

She paused for a deep, trembling breath and pressed her palms together, bringing them up against her lips. "Anyway, things were great for a while, but then I lost my job. I applied at every station in Tucson, but no one would hire me. Finally, I got an offer from a station in Detroit. He didn't want to move, so ...."

"You left," Kyle said softly.

She nodded. When had he taken her hand? She couldn't remember. But she realized he was holding it now, gently massaging her knuckles with his thumb.

"We tried to keep the marriage together. We visited back and forth on weekends every three or four weeks. Every penny we earned went to the airlines or the phone company. It worked out fine for several months, but then he missed a visit. Then another. He started having all kinds of excuses why he couldn't come, why I shouldn't come to see him. Business problems. This and that.

"Finally, I discovered he was seeing someone else. It hurt so much. I was heartbroken. I was lonely, too, but I hadn't cheated on him. Then he called me one night ... he didn't even have the decency to tell me in person. He wanted to marry her. He wanted a divorce."

"I'm sorry." A brief silence fell, then he said: "I understand why you had to leave, to go where the work was. But why wasn't he willing to move with you?"

"He was only licensed to practice law in Arizona. He'd

built up a clientele. How could he leave? When it comes down to it, one person in a marriage has to be willing to move, sometimes to sacrifice their career if need be for the other. And I don't think that's fair to either one of them."

Which is why I can never marry again, she wanted to say. But somehow, she couldn't bring herself to voice the words aloud.

His arms tightened suddenly around her. "I think when two people love each other enough, no matter what, they can find a way to be together."

"It's not always so simple."

"It can be." He stroked her back and shoulders as he hugged her, while rocking the swing back and forth. She clung to him and buried her face against his neck.

"I don't want to go through that again," she whispered, knowing at the same time that she couldn't bear to let him go. "I'm not strong enough. It took years for my heart to knit itself back together, for me to realize I could survive on my own."

His lips moved over her shoulder, her neck, and she felt herself succumbing to his magic touch. "Desiree, you were hurt badly, I know, and I'm so very sorry. But you've got to let go of the past. What happened to you before isn't going to happen to us. It's not going to be easy … nothing worth having ever is. But we can't throw this away. Not before we've even tried."

He drew back and cradled her face in his hands, adding: "Give us time, sweetheart. Give us a chance to make things work."

Her eyes brimming with tears, she slid her hands around his neck and pressed her lips against his. His kiss was a warm, sure force. She felt his strength pouring into her body, filling her, making her new.

Maybe, just maybe she was wrong. Maybe, somehow, they *could* make things work. At the moment she couldn't imagine how, but what did it matter?

How could she possibly say goodbye to him, even if she wanted to?

"SIGN HERE, PLEASE." The burly deliveryman extended a clipboard and Desiree dutifully signed her name.

It was Tuesday morning. Kyle had left before sunrise the day before, and Desiree had spent the day and night reliving their long weekend over and over in her mind, her body still tingling from the memory of his touch.

He'd called her at the station Monday afternoon, and again late that night when neither of them could sleep. They'd teased and tantalized each other over the phone with vivid descriptions of what they'd be doing if they were together. It had taken hours to fall asleep.

"You'd better let me carry this in for you," the deliveryman said. "It's pretty heavy."

A good five minutes later, she finally managed to pry open the top of the large, heavy carton. She turned the box to its side, pulled out the contents, and stood it upright on the hardwood floor.

It was a chair. A delicately carved mahogany chair with a straight back and a steel-blue, floral tapestry seat, the kind that would be at home in a long line of matching chairs in an elegant, nineteenth-century dining room.

She loved it on sight. The smooth grain was stained a deep reddish color, the same shade as her credenza. He must have seen it in an antique shop and known how much she'd like it. What a unique gift! How thoughtful! She ran her fingers along the highly polished rung across the back, touched to her very soul.

That afternoon, the hot line flashed in her control room at the station. Her heart leapt when she heard his voice.

"Hi, sweetheart. Miss me?"

"Yes! Oh, Kyle, the chair ... it arrived this morning. How did you ever get it here so fast? I don't know how to—"

"Do you like it?"

"I love it! It's exquisite. Thank you."

"You're welcome. I wanted to make sure you liked it before I send the other one."

"What other one?"

"You can't just have one chair, for God's sake. It's a matched set or nothing." He chuckled. "I've got to run. I only had a minute between meetings. See you Friday night, right? Let's eat in. Can you cook?"

"What?"

"I asked if you can cook. The only things I've eaten made by your two hands are a freshly squeezed orange, an English muffin, and a salad."

She laughed. "I can cook."

"Great. I'm dying for a home-cooked meal. And I'm dying to hold you in my arms. I'll see you at the airport. Bye."

She smiled at the phone long after he'd hung up. "He's crazy," she muttered to herself. "Absolutely crazy."

~

IT TOOK three-quarters of an hour for two deliverymen to set up the new dining-room table and five additional chairs Friday morning. The note that accompanied them read:

I hope you love this. If not, no worries, we can send it back. Love, Kyle

P.S. I hope your great-grandmother would have approved.

Opened to its full oblong size with the two accompanying leaves, the gleaming mahogany table stretched majestically across the room. Everything about the table reminded her of Kyle. Its strength. Its beauty. Its polished sophistication.

She knew she shouldn't accept such an expensive gift, but she couldn't send it back, either. It blended perfectly with her other furniture and suited the house as if made for it.

No wonder he wanted to eat in tonight, she thought with a grin as she frosted a dark chocolate layer cake later that morning. She popped a leg of lamb into the oven—his favorite meal, he'd told her, lobster notwithstanding—and set the timer to start baking at four o'clock.

After closing the table to a small oval, she covered it with the only tablecloth she possessed, and set out her best china.

When she picked him up at the airport after work, they flew into each other's arms as if separated five months instead of only five days. The aroma of succulent roast lamb enveloped her senses as they opened her front door, and he closed his eyes, savoring the delicious scent.

When they finished eating, he proclaimed it the best meal he'd ever tasted, and promptly whisked the chef off to bed to show his appreciation.

The nights were long with loving, the days warm and fun-filled and far too short. Each morning they exercised and jogged. On Saturday they toured the immense *Queen Mary* and Howard Hughes's *Spruce Goose,* docked at San Pedro harbor.

They wandered through the quaint Cape Cod-style harborside shops at Ports of Call Village, where Kyle bought her hand-woven Irish linen tablecloths to fit the table in two different sizes. They had dinner aboard the elegant *Princess Louise,* a cruise ship turned restaurant, and toasted a passing tugboat with raised glasses of icy champagne.

On Sunday they rented bikes and rode along the meandering paths at a large tree-shaded park a few miles from her house, then returned home with sunburned shoulders and noses.

They made love in the hushed stillness of early evening, the setting sun glowing on their bodies through the open bedroom windows.

"I'm hungry," she said much, much later, as they lay face-to-face on the plush area rug in her living room, each wearing nothing but a smile. "I feel like I haven't eaten in four days."

The brass table lamps on either side of her couch cast a warm glow on the frosty glass of iced tea they sipped together through separate straws.

"It's no wonder, after all the strenuous activity we've had this weekend," he said.

"Are you referring to daytime activity or nighttime?"

"Take your pick."

She laughed. "How many calories do you think we burned up last night? I should go check my scale. I've probably lost five pounds by now."

"Don't get too excited. You're going to gain it all back at dinner. What I have in mind is sinfully fattening." He kissed her, then jumped to his feet and disappeared into the kitchen.

"There's nothing decent in the refrigerator, unless you want leftover leg of lamb. We ate everything else for breakfast."

"I know," he called from the other room. "Let's order something in."

"Great!" A sudden craving seized her, and her mouth began to water. *A thick, Sicilian-style pizza oozing with sauce and cheese, smothered with ....*

She frowned, shook her head. No. Not his style. A man who serves pâté and champagne and chocolate mousse on a beach picnic, who orders *canard a l'orange* and *salade Lyonnaise* in their native tongue, will not go for an everything-on-it pizza.

He returned with the Yellow Pages. Kneeling down beside her, he opened the book on the coffee table and flipped through it. "Is there a place around here that makes a nice, juicy pizza with a thick crust? I always go for The Works, but what do you like? Mushroom? Sausage? Olives? Pepperoni?"

At her astonished expression he added, "What? Don't you like pizza?" His eyes narrowed and he wagged his index finger at her. "It's un-American not to like pizza."

She burst out laughing and threw her arms around his neck. "I adore pizza! I was afraid to admit it. I thought you only liked gourmet food."

"There's a time and a place for gourmet food, and a time and a place for junk food."

"That is so profound." She kissed him, still laughing. "Want to hear a secret? I'm a closet junk-food junkie."

His arms glided around her waist. "Really? A chocoholic *and* a junk-food junkie? I'm impressed. What's your favorite?"

"My favorite what?" Her hands combed adoringly through the silky short hair at the back of his neck.

"Junk food."

"Oh!" Her lips followed the movements of her fingers. "Well, a Big Mac of course. They put the greatest sauce on those things. And of course, hot salty fries and a chocolate shake."

She spread kisses down his neck, across his shoulder. His breath hissed in through his teeth. "That's your favorite?"

"Yes ... no, wait. Big Macs are my second favorite. My first favorite are S'mores. How I used to *love* those."

He pulled her more closely against him. "S'mores?"

"Yes." She settled against him, loving the feel of his strong arms around her, the warmth of his skin. "We used to make them on Girl Scout camping trips."

His mouth and tongue paid an inordinate amount of attention to the soft skin behind her ear, and she gasped, arched her neck, and closed her eyes as she struggled to continue. "You ... toast marshmallows over the campfire until they're hot and gooey, then squish them between two graham crackers and a square of chocolate. The … hot marshmallow makes the chocolate melt …." Sort of like *she* was melting right now. "They call them that because they're so good, you always want S'more."

"I know."

"You do?"

He nodded. "We used to make them in Boy Scouts. I haven't had one in eons." Cradling her back over his arm, his mouth charted a fiery trail down her neck to the valley between her breasts.

"What's your favorite?" she murmured throatily.

"My favorite?" His hand slid up the outside of her thigh, then swept over the curve of her hip to cup her bare bosom. "I always like a nice juicy … breast."

"I presume you mean … a chicken breast?"

"Presume all you like."

"That's not a junk food," she pointed out hazily.

"It's not? What were we talking about? I got distracted." His lips closed around the object of his affection and he lowered her to the soft carpet.

"Kyle. Wait. The pizza … you forgot to order the pizza."

"The pizza can wait." He covered her with his warm, hard body. "Right now," he whispered huskily, "I want S'more."

BEFORE SUNRISE MONDAY morning he sat on the edge of her bed, dressed in a dark blue three-piece suit as he kissed her goodbye.

"I wish you'd let me take you to the airport," she said as she held him fiercely against her chest.

"There's no point. You'd only be stuck in morning traffic." He stood up. "I've got a busy week of negotiations coming up. I may not have time to call every night."

"Okay."

"I'll miss you."

"I'll miss you." She couldn't stop the tears that trickled down her cheeks. Damn! She didn't want to cry every time he left, didn't want him to see her this way.

He leaned down and kissed her again. "I need you, Desiree," he whispered. She watched him go through a blur of tears.

It was the longest week of her life. She bought a stack of cards at a stationery store and sent him one each morning. On Tuesday she sent him a cuddly, stuffed toy lobster of plush red velour, which she found in a children's boutique. *I'm hungry for you*, her note read.

She didn't hear from him all day. When she tried calling him at the office, his secretary said he was tied up in meetings, and he didn't return her call.

Wednesday, she had a mixed flower arrangement sent to his office, with a note saying, *Let's do business together*. She called him that afternoon, but their conversation was cut short soon after he thanked her for the flowers.

"I'm sorry I haven't called, honey," he explained. "I've been wining and dining clients all week. I'm in the middle of negotiations for an important contract and I just don't have time to talk."

She sat on the edge of her bed Thursday night, fresh from a shower, about to apply polish to the second to last toenail, when the phone rang. She jumped to her feet and grabbed the receiver, the nail-polish brush still in her hand.

"Hi, lover." The deep vibrant voice never ceased to send delicious shivers up her spine.

She smiled radiantly into the receiver. "Hi. I miss you. I can't wait to see you tomorrow."

"I miss you, too. And thanks for the stuffed lobster. Didn't do a thing for my appetite, but he's cute." He paused. "Listen, Desiree. I've got bad news."

Her stomach tensed. The radiant smile disappeared. "What's wrong?"

"I expected these negotiations to wrap up today, or by noon tomorrow at the latest, in time for me to catch my flight. But there's no way that's going to happen. The client refuses to budge on his price, and I'm not going to give this thing away. We need at least three, maybe four more days. They've got a bunch of guys here from Cleveland who don't want to fly home for the weekend and come right back. We've agreed to work Saturday and Sunday to get this thing done."

"Oh." She sank down onto the bed. A hot flash of disappointment coursed through her, touching every limb, every nerve.

She tried to stab the nail-polish brush back into the mouth of the tiny bottle, missed, and stabbed again. The bottle tipped over and rolled off the nightstand, trailing Passion Pink along the hardwood floor into the bathroom. Tears of hurt and frustration burned behind her eyes.

"I'm sorry, sweetheart. The last thing I wanted was to spend the weekend locked up in a conference room, haggling with a bunch of businessmen. But I have no choice. I'd like to turn it over to my negotiating team, but I've got two new people and I can't afford any screw-ups. The deal's too important. Please don't be angry."

"I'm not angry." She was just sad. Steve's excuses for not coming to see her were always just as crucial, just as plausible, and always at the last minute. She had believed him right up to the bitter end.

In the past week apart, did Kyle come to see the futility of their relationship? Was this his way of letting her down softly? *No*, her brain insisted. He was telling the truth. He had to be. Two tears trickled down her cheeks and she sniffed.

"Hey. Hey," he said softly. "It's only one weekend. I'll be there next Friday, on the same flight I planned to take today. All right? You'll meet me?"

"I'll meet you."

They were silent for a moment. She clutched at one last hope. "What about the manufacturing plant you were looking at down here?" At least if he buys it, she thought, he'll have to fly down here once in a while. "What did you decide?"

"The prospects didn't look good. I decided against it. I'm looking at a company in Tulsa, Oklahoma, instead. I have to fly out there next week."

She stifled a gasp of disappointment. Tulsa, Oklahoma. What if he met another woman while he was there? Would he spend the weekend with her? *Don't be ridiculous*, she told herself. *He cares for you!*

When he spoke again his voice was low, deep, rusty. "Desiree, I miss you. I can't begin to tell you how much. I'm sorry I can't be there tomorrow, but I'll make it up to you. I promise."

They said goodbye, and Desiree knelt down, retrieved the half-empty bottle of polish, and began to clean up the spill. *I promise.* How many times had she heard those two words from Steve? Promises were so easily made, and so easily broken ....

She shook her head firmly, determined not to let such gloomy thoughts take over her mind. It was just one weekend, not the end of the world. This was Kyle, not Steve. They would get through this. Everything was going to be okay.

She found solace and pleasure in reading and working in her garden, pursuits she had always thoroughly enjoyed on her own before she met him. But somehow, they were no longer quite as enjoyable.

Each time the phone rang she jumped to answer it, disappointment piercing through her with razor sharpness when it wasn't Kyle.

You'll see him Friday, she reminded herself. *He will come.*

She got through the next day at work, and the next. Her calm voice and brittle smile masked the lonely ache that wrenched at her heart. Wednesday night he still hadn't called.

She lay down on the bed and closed her eyes, her mind full of vivid memories of their lovemaking. The room echoed with remembered laughter, electric touches, softly whispered endearments.

She blinked open her eyes, wishing she could make him

magically appear in the doorway. But the doorway was empty.

From that moment at Catalina Island when she'd first acknowledged her burgeoning love for him, the feeling had grown and blossomed until every filament of her being seemed to shine with newly found sustenance from within.

She felt as if he was her missing other half, a part of herself she hadn't even known had been lacking.

Could she ever again feel completely happy or whole without his warmth, his caring, his sharing? She doubted it.

Yet she still didn't know if he loved her. She could see deep affection in his eyes every time he looked at her, feel it in his touch every time they made love. But he'd never said the words.

Did he love her? Could there be any kind of future for the two of them? Or would it always be like this ... a few glorious weekends, with long stretches of lonely disappointment in between?

Why? Why? she asked herself silently as she covered her face with her hands. *Why did I do this to myself again?*

Why did I let myself fall so deeply, so hopelessly in love with him, when I knew this would happen?

"When I said I wanted a hot and sizzling evening," Desiree said into the mike, "I wasn't referring to the temperature outside."

She mustered every ounce of vigor to spice up her voice. "Let's hope the thermometer takes a nosedive in the next hour or so because this city is sweltering. Right now, it's ten minutes before six o'clock on this Thursday afternoon and I'm Desiree, getting ready to sign off. Coming up is Dave Hamilton and thirty minutes of non-stop music on KICK 102. Catch you tomorrow, same time, same place."

Pulling off the headphones, she stood up and wearily shook out her long curls. She filled in the broadcast log with all the promos she'd played and did a little end-of-the-day housecleaning in the studio, then cued up an especially long, sentimental love song which matched her mood.

Slumping on the stool, she toyed with the frayed edge of her cutoffs and closed her eyes as the lyrical, feminine voice sang out softly, sadly:

"We're on opposite shores, but lover I'm yours, Come take me away ... I'm lost in your arms, fall prey to your charms, when you hold me that way ...."

The studio door opened. "Hi," he said softly.

"Kyle." She realized she'd whispered his name aloud, heard agonized relief in her voice as she jumped off the stool and threw herself into his arms.

Desiree opened her eyes. The room was as empty and lifeless as before. She breathed in deeply and shut her eyes again, losing herself in the scene that unfolded in her imagination:

He took her in his embrace, capturing her mouth with his.

"I've thought of nothing but you since I left. I could hardly eat. Sleep." He covered her face and neck with kisses. "I've missed you so much. I missed holding you, touching you. I couldn't forget what you feel like. It tormented me, day and night."

A delicious warmth penetrated her body. She hugged

her arms to her chest as the soft, sweet words of the song swam around her, through her:

"I tremble like a child, a fire burning wild, you bring out the woman in me ...."

His mouth feasted on hers. Their tongues met, skirmished. She tightened her arms around his neck and swayed against him.

He reached down with two hands, undid the snap and zipper of her cutoffs. In a few swift movements, he removed the clothing between them and pulled her down to the floor with him.

She gasped but made no move to protest. At his lightest touch she shuddered with desire.

"I want you so badly, I love you so madly, take me now and set me free ...."

The studio door flew open. "Move over, gorgeous, it's my turn."

Desiree blinked, refocusing glazed eyes as she struggled to return reluctantly to the present. Dave, the slightly balding deejay on the evening shift, towered above her.

"Were you asleep?" he asked.

"No. Just ... daydreaming."

"You've been off in a fog ever since the first day that boyfriend of yours showed up in his fancy Maserati."

"I have not," she replied defensively.

"The point is not up for discussion." With a sidelong glance at the promo log on the counter, he added, "Good thing you've been filling this thing in. Can't afford any mistakes now."

She slid off the stool, grabbed her purse, and leaned against the counter, her mind still in a daze. "Why? What do you mean?"

"Didn't you hear? Old man Westler is planning to put this place up for sale. Retire."

She snapped back to reality now with full force. "For sale? When?"

"Don't know. He hasn't made any announcements yet. It's just a rumor going around. But I've found *that* kind of rumor usually turns out to be true."

A wave of fear flooded her body. New owners were notorious for doing major overhauls, firing everyone and starting over from scratch. She bit her lip. "I was miserable enough without hearing that kind of news, Dave."

"Well, cheer up. It might not happen, and if it does, let's hope we both get to stay. Right now, it's time for you to split, so git." He sank onto the stool and picked up the headphones. Jerking his thumb over his shoulder, he added, "By the way, there's something waiting for you in the parking lot."

She stared at him blankly. "Something waiting for me? What?"

Dave waved an impatient arm, "Go see for yourself, woman!" He flashed her a knowing smile. "I'll give you one little hint. It's not a Maserati."

CHAPTER 10

Desiree punched open the studio door. What was waiting for her in the parking lot? If it wasn't Kyle, then who or what could it be?

She raced down the hall and through the reception area, then threw open the double glass exterior doors. The dry heat seared her skin after the air-conditioned interior of the station. She turned the corner of the building to the asphalt parking lot, then stopped dead in her tracks.

Parked across and in front of her car and three others, a sleek, white Cadillac stretch limousine gleamed in the late afternoon sun. A tall man in a dark suit stood beside it, his hand resting on the back door handle.

"Ohh!" she cried aloud. What did Kyle do? Send a limo to take her to the airport, so she'd fly up to see him? But ... she couldn't go. It was Thursday. She had to work tomorrow.

She took a few tentative steps forward.

"Miss Germain?" the man asked.

She nodded. He opened the door, gestured for her to step inside.

The hell with it, she decided. Be spontaneous. Respond to the moment!

She flew to the door, bent down, and slid inside onto a soft, leather seat. Long arms immediately scooped her up, drawing her against a broad chest, and warm, familiar lips came down on hers.

Desiree's eyes opened wide with surprise and met Kyle's twinkling green ones. She let out a cry of pleasure as her arms came up around his neck.

Vaguely she heard the car door shut, another door open, and the motor start as Kyle hooked a hand under her legs, lifted her across his lap, and settled her between his thighs.

"What are you doing here, you crazy man?" she whispered against his lips.

"I couldn't wait until tomorrow." His mouth rained kisses across her cheeks. "I couldn't stay away another day."

They kissed long and deeply, holding each other tightly, drinking of each other as if dying of thirst. The car moved forward. She ran her hands across his wide shoulders, his back, his ribs, reacquainting herself with each hard, familiar muscle, bone, and sinew.

"I missed you," she whispered when she was able. "I missed you so much, I thought I'd die."

His hands roved her body, slipped under her snug-fitting T-shirt, to glide up the smooth, soft flesh of her back. "I'm sorry I wasn't here last weekend. I'm sorry I haven't called. I came straight from Tulsa. I've been there all week, negotiating a major contract. I barely had time to eat or sleep."

"I'm so glad you're here." She hugged him. Hard. "I'm sorry if I sounded upset that night on the phone. I was just so disappointed. I wanted you so much."

"I wanted you, too." He kissed her again, then cuddled her against him.

"How long can you stay?"

"Only tonight."

She tilted her head back, mouth opening in dismay. His dark brown hair was perfectly combed, and he looked even more handsome than she remembered. "You flew down here for just one night?"

He nodded. "I left the negotiations to the rest of the team this afternoon. Looks like things will wrap tomorrow in Tulsa, so I'm heading back to Seattle first thing in the morning."

She sighed sadly, then leaned her head on his shoulder, wrapping her arms around his chest. "I won't think about it right now. I'm going to enjoy every precious minute we've got."

She took a moment to glance about the interior of the car. Wide, leather seats faced each other across an expanse of grey carpet. A small television was built into the textured leather wall on one side, along with a stereo receiver.

Above it, a tiny bar held a row of crystal glasses engraved with the Cadillac logo. A phone hung on the opposite wall, beside a magazine rack. The green neck of a bottle poked out from an ice bucket at their feet.

"This is incredible," she breathed, then turned to him.

"You remembered what I said that night, didn't you? About the limo?"

"I did."

She glanced down at her denim cutoffs and lavender T-shirt, which was silk-screened with the KICK logo in black and silver. "I'm so underdressed. If I'd known I was going to ride in a limousine tonight, I would have worn my electric-blue silk dress."

"You mean the one that's—"

"Cut just off the shoulder, terribly chic," they sang out in unison. It had become a standing joke with them, and they laughed.

"Don't worry. For what we're about to do, you're dressed perfectly."

For the first time, she noticed that he wasn't wearing his usual tailored business suit. Instead, he'd dressed casually, in a polo shirt and blue jeans that fit like old friends—snug across the hips, and whitewashed at the seams and pocket edges. His running shoes looked well-worn, white fading into gray.

Her eyes narrowed curiously. "Where are we going?"

"You'll see. This night is for you." He squeezed her hand. "You're going to see all your fantasies come true."

"All my fantasies?" she repeated in amusement.

He nodded, grinning. "First, a stop at your favorite restaurant."

There were two or three elegant restaurants in the area that she was particularly fond of, but she didn't remember specifying a favorite, and they were underdressed for any of them. Since he refused to elaborate, she sank back into the seat with a resigned sigh and enjoyed the ride.

A few minutes later, the limousine pulled up to a McDonald's and parked in front of the door.

"You've got to be kidding!" she squealed, nudging him in the ribs. "A limo to take us to McDonald's?"

He just grinned with delight.

The driver stepped to her side of the car, opened the door, and helped her out. Once inside, Kyle ordered five Big Macs, three large orders of fries, and two chocolate shakes.

"Someone's joining us?" she asked.

"No, it's just the two of us. You did say all these were your favorites?"

She nodded with helpless laughter. "I did."

"I don't want you to go hungry. Anything else?"

"No, thank you. This'll do just fine."

A pleasant-looking man with silvery hair stepped in through the door, accompanied by a woman of about the same age. They both looked over their shoulders. "Whose do you think it is?" the man whispered, gesturing toward the waiting limousine.

The woman searched the faces in the crowded room as they stepped behind Kyle and Desiree in line. "I don't know. I don't recognize anyone famous. Seems funny to see it here. Maybe—"

"Look no further." Kyle put his arm around Desiree and faced the couple with a charming smile. "No famous faces here tonight, folks, just a famous voice. This is Desiree Germain from KICK-102 FM."

Desiree felt her knees grow weak. Famous voice? She wanted to sink into the floor and disappear. But to her surprise, the man's eyes widened with recognition and apparent admiration.

"No kidding? You're Desiree?" The man clapped his hands together. "Well, what do you know. I listen to you all the time!"

"So do I," said the woman at his side, who was now beaming with excitement. "And so does our son. He loves your show."

Desiree's face lit up with a heartfelt smile. Instinctively, she held out her hand. "Thank you. It's so nice to meet you."

The man shook her hand with enthusiasm. "I'm honored to meet *you*. Really honored. Wait until Ron hears about this!" He grabbed a napkin from the dispenser on the counter and pulled a pen out of his pocket. "Would you autograph this for—for my son Ron, please?"

"Sure. And what are your names?"

"Roy," the man answered.

"Joy," replied the woman.

Desiree wrote, *For Roy, Joy, and Ron. Life's a KICK at 102 FM. With all best wishes, Desiree.*

The couple were clearly thrilled. Several other people came forward and clamored for her autograph. It seemed as if she'd signed a dozen paper napkins when Kyle finally grabbed her arm and steered her out the door with their bags of food.

She leaned back against the seat, incredulous, as the limo pulled away. "I can't believe you told them who I was."

"Why? You're a celebrity. Don't tell me no one's ever asked for your autograph before."

"Only a few times. People don't usually recognize me by

my voice. And I don't go around introducing myself so brazenly, the way you did."

"You should. It'd be great publicity."

Where had she heard that before? Barbara. The day the woman from some restaurant had called and asked her to emcee their opening party. Suddenly Desire wanted to do that kind of party, lots of parties, wanted to get out and meet the people who listened to her on the radio.

"I feel so fantastic when you're here," she cried happily. "You make me feel like anything is possible."

His eyes shone with tender admiration. "Only because it is."

The driver took them to the mile-wide, tree-shaded park where they'd ridden bicycles two weeks before. Kyle handed the McDonald's bags to Desiree. He pulled a bulky canvas bag out of the trunk, threw the strap over his shoulder, and grabbed the ice bucket.

"We'll be back in a while," he told the driver. "I hope you brought a good book to read."

The driver chuckled and signaled goodbye with a courteous wave.

Kyle put his arm around Desiree and gave her a squeeze. "Follow me."

The sun hung low in the sky, bathing the lush green lawns on either side of the bike path in warm, golden light. They followed the path until it curved around a small lake and climbed up a short hillside to a grassy knoll.

He stopped beside a picnic table and set down the canvas bag. A cement fire ring stood in a clearing a few yards away.

Kyle pulled out a red plaid blanket and shook it open. "I

hope you like dining alfresco. This spot was crucial for phase two of my plan."

"Phase two?"

"You'll see."

"You *always* say that." Desiree helped him spread the blanket on the grass. "Well, if your Picnic in the Park is anything like your Day at the Beach, I'll *really* be impressed."

"Oh yeah?"

"You're a master of creativity when it comes to picnics. Not to mention other out-of-door ... activities."

Laughing huskily, he put his arms around her and drew her close. She met the warm look in his eyes, and felt her throat constrict with an overpowering rush of affection.

"It's been a long two weeks, hasn't it?" he whispered.

"It seemed like two years." Her heart pounded as his lips nuzzled the softly curling hair at the side of her neck. She wanted to melt against him, to wrap her arms around his neck, to tell him how much he meant to her.

Kyle, I love you, she wanted to say. But was this the right time? Would he feel pressured to admit to the same depth of feeling, or think she expected some sort of commitment in return? Before she could speak, his mouth came to hers in a quick, urgent kiss, and he withdrew.

"Let's eat while it's still lukewarm," he said gruffly. He grabbed the bags of food and sat down on the blanket.

Desiree took a deep breath, dropped down beside him, and crossed her legs, managing a smile. "Right. Let's eat."

The sun had descended below the treetops and the sky had turned a pale dusky grey by the time they finished the milkshakes, consumed two hamburgers each, and ate most of the French fries.

Several yards below them, a flock of ducks gathered at the water's edge, bobbing about expectantly.

"Let's throw them a hamburger bun," Kyle suggested.

Desiree plucked off the top bun from the remaining burger and scrambled down the incline. Kyle followed. They both ripped the bun into small pieces and tossed them into the water near the shore.

The ducks made grateful noises as they darted toward the food. When they'd flung them the last piece, Desiree raised her palms. "Sorry. All gone." Disappointed, the ducks turned tail and glided away across the silent water.

Kyle took Desiree's hand in his and led her back up the slope. "Okay. Main course is finished. Leftovers dutifully disposed of. Now, for dessert."

Drawing out several small logs from the canvas bag, he arranged them in a pile inside the nearby cement fire ring, on top of the paper trash from their dinner.

"A campfire?" she murmured, crouching down beside him. "How nice."

Casting her a mischievous grin, he lit the fire and fanned it to life. All at once she realized what he must be up to, and she drew an astonished breath.

"S'mores?" she cried. "But how—"

"Phase two of Your Fantasies Come True." Kyle dug out additional items from the canvas bag and placed each one in her arms with a flourish. "One bag of marshmallows. One box of honey graham crackers. Two extra-large chocolate bars. And two extra-long toasting forks."

She laughed her delight and would have hugged him if

her arms hadn't been full. "You are amazing. But you said it's been ages since you had these. How did you remember the ingredients?"

His eyes twinkled. "A loyal Boy Scout never forgets how to make a S'more."

A refreshing summer breeze blew across the lake, cooling the evening air. They sat close together on the hard-packed earth, toasting handfuls of marshmallows to a golden brown over the glowing embers, and then squeezing them and squares of chocolate between two graham crackers.

When he pressed the crackers too hard, she leaned forward and licked the molten white goo that squeezed out the sides. They laughed, kissed, and passed the sweet confections back and forth until their hands were sticky and their faces were streaked with charcoal.

"Happy?" Kyle asked when they'd consumed as much as they could stand. Darkness was fast approaching now. The park was lit only by the last rays of sunlight and the glow of a few well-placed pole lamps. "Feel indecently indulged?"

"I do," she sighed contentedly.

"Good." He brought her back to the blanket and pulled her down beside him. "It's time now to indulge one of my fantasies: sipping Perrier Jouet in the park at sunset with the girl of my dreams."

He withdrew a slender bottle from the ice bucket, then proceeded to open it. Delicate white flowers were hand painted on the dark green grass. Desiree knew an expensive bottle of champagne when she saw one. "Wow, this must be a special occasion."

"It is. It's the three-week anniversary of the day we met." He retrieved a champagne glass from the bucket, filled it, and lifted it to her lips. She sipped.

"Mmmmm. Delicious."

He brought the glass to his own lips and drank. Their eyes met and never wavered as they passed the glass back and forth, slowly finishing the tangy bubbling wine.

Her heartbeat performed an erratic dance and she felt all at once enveloped in tenderness; it seemed as if her very soul would melt under the endearing affection that she saw glowing in his eyes.

He set the glass aside, and murmuring her name, he collected her in his arms and sealed her mouth with his.

Warmth spread through her body like wildfire as she wrapped her arms around him, answering his kiss with all the fevered urgency in her heart. They sank down on the blanket and rolled to their sides, clinging together, mouth against mouth, tongue meeting tongue, her softness molding against his hard strength. His hands roamed down her back, then up again to her shoulders as her hands tangled in his hair.

She swallowed his kisses like nectar, each kiss alternately filling her and increasing her thirst until she felt almost limp with desire. She lost pace with her breath, her blood spinning through veins that seemed delighted to swell and pump.

Through the layers of their clothes, she felt the heat of his body and of his desire, and that part of her which sought him throbbed in joyous response.

When at last he spoke, his voice was deep and rusty, caressing in its warm intensity.

"Desiree, I love you."

Tears welled in her eyes. She held him to her, wanting to heighten their contact, to prolong it for all eternity. "I love you, too," she whispered.

He kissed her again, long and lovingly, his hands stroking her hair. "If you only knew how much I've longed to say those words aloud. I fell in love with you the night we met. The very first night."

"So did I," she murmured against his lips. "I've wanted to tell you for such a long time, but I was afraid—"

"Afraid of what?" He smoothed the hair back from her forehead. "That I didn't feel as strongly about you as you did about me?"

She nodded. A tear spilled from her eye to trickle down her cheek as she saw his answering nod, and she understood that he'd harbored the same fears.

"It seems we've been holding back our feelings to no purpose." He smiled warmly, tracing a fingertip across her lips. "But there's nothing to stop me from saying it now. I love you, Desiree. With all my heart. I love you."

A radiant smile curved her lips, and she pressed her mouth against his in a soft kiss. "I love you," she whispered. "I love you. I love you. I love you!"

She punctuated each tender admission with a kiss at the corners of his lips, on his chin, his nose, his eyes, his forehead. She rested her cheek against his, slowly drew it across the scratchy pull of his day's growth of beard, then covered the roughened skin with small kisses.

The depth of her emotions coursed through her, filling her with such joy that she couldn't help laughing out loud. He hugged her to him, laughing in return. It felt so good to have him here, so wonderful to be in his arms, so right to be able to show—and voice—her love this way.

He rolled her to her back and cupped one of her hands in his. Bringing her fingers to his lips, he gazed down at her, his eyes a mirror of the love she knew must be shining within her own.

"I don't want to leave you, ever again," he said. "Not even for a day. I want to share the rest of my life with you, to have you by my side, with me always.

"Desiree, will you be my wife? Will you marry me?"

CHAPTER 11

Ten seconds dragged by as Desiree lay still beneath him, her mind in a whirl of confusion. His proposal astonished, flattered, and thrilled her all at the same time.

On the one hand, she wanted to jump to her feet and shout, *Of course I'll marry you!* But on the heels of this joyous possibility tread the painful wrench of reality, keeping her earthbound.

"I love you," she said finally, as she reached up to caress his cheek. "More than I'll ever love anyone. And I would love to be your wife. But how can we get married? Where would we live?"

"That's something we'll have to figure out. Would you consider moving to Seattle?"

Disappointment coursed through her. She could hardly believe he was asking her this. All the times they'd discussed this dreaded subject, hadn't he been listening? She rolled out from under him and sat up with a sigh.

"Kyle, we've talked about this. You know how important my career is to me. I—"

"I know," he cut in, "and—"

"Wait, let me finish. Let me explain. I've wanted to be a deejay ever since my seventh birthday, when my grandpa gave me my first transistor radio. I used to lie awake at night, dreaming up the things I'd say and do on the air. My voice is my biggest asset. The personality I've created on radio is an important part of me. Radio is my *life*. I couldn't give it up."

Kyle sat up and grasped both her hands earnestly in his. "Desiree, I respect your talent. I admire you. Don't you realize that? Your career means as much to me as it does to you. I'd *never* want you to give it up. Never."

"But I'd have to if I married you."

"Why? That's ridiculous. Why can't you have both marriage and a career? I know this is a lot to ask, since you're doing so well here. You have fans ... boy do you have fans!" He grinned, and she knew he was thinking of the scene earlier in McDonald's.

"But a talent like yours should be welcome in Seattle— at the right station, anyway. Especially after the rave reviews you've gotten lately in the newspaper."

"You might think so, but it's not that easy. Good jobs like mine are hard to find, and even harder for women. And I have definite goals for myself. Someday I'd like to do animation, voice-overs, commercials. Southern California's the best market for that."

He frowned. "Seattle might be a smaller market, but I'm sure you could find those opportunities there. And in five years, maybe ten, who knows? You might even find your-self managing a station."

"That'd be great," she admitted. "I'd love to have that kind of control. But the basic problem *now* still remains. As a radio jock, no matter where I'm working, there's no guarantee how long it will last. Even if we start out in the same city, at some point I'd have to move away."

"That's a bridge we'll cross if we come to it. It's no reason not to get married."

She chewed her lower lip pensively. Was he right? Had she been clinging to that same, old excuse far too long? Was it time to move forward, to take a risk, to believe in the possibility of a future together?

Suddenly, she remembered what Dave had told her at the station earlier that day. "Kyle: I forgot to tell you. My station might be up for sale."

"Really? Why?"

"The owner, Adam Westler, bought the place as sort of a hobby. He made his money years ago in something else. Oil, I think. If he sells, there's no telling what will happen to me or anyone else at KICK. The new owner might not be so keen on female deejays. I could be out of a job in two seconds."

A grin spread across Kyle's face. "That's great! Then you'd have no reason to stay down here."

Desiree batted his arm playfully. "Hey, I'm talking about being fired. Whose side are you on?"

"Our side. I just want us to be together. I say, find another job fast, before the station changes hands. You'll get a far better offer from another station if you have a good job behind you."

"I doubt it'll make any difference. Wages are tops here. There's no way any station in Seattle could come close to matching my salary."

"Who gives a damn about salary? I make more money than we will ever need. I'm talking about the *job*, the drive-time shift you want so badly."

"It'd be nothing short of a miracle if I was offered a drive-time shift in Seattle. I've never been there. I don't know anyone in the business."

"But I do."

"You do?"

He nodded. "I've done some heavy radio advertising for Sparkle Light in the past year." He laid her hand across his thigh and stroked it with gentle fingers.

"I've been thinking about this for the past few weeks—I hope you don't mind. I know you would have done it on your own, but I took the liberty of making a few phone calls. I thought if I set something up, it would move things along that much faster."

Her eyebrows shot up. "And?"

"Unfortunately, the first two stations I tried aren't hiring right now …."

"You see?" She heaved a sigh.

"But!" he interjected. "Ed Alder, the program director at KXTR in Seattle, is on the lookout for new talent. And: he'd like to meet you."

"He would?"

Kyle nodded. "Do you have an audition tape?"

Her heart beat faster. "Yes. It's about a year old, but still pretty good."

"Would you like me to deliver it to him? Do you want to fly up for an interview?"

"I suppose I could—"

"Fantastic!" He drew her to her feet, squeezed her hands excitedly. "I'll give you the grand tour of Seattle. I'll even set up a dinner at my parents' house. You can meet my family. I've told them all about you. They're dying to meet you."

"Your family? Oh, no!" She laughed. "This is sounding more and more official by the minute."

"It *is* official." His arms encircled her waist and he kissed her soundly. "How soon can you get away? Can you fly back with me tomorrow?"

"Tomorrow?" She laughed again, caught up in his enthusiasm. But then, a worrisome thought followed. Even if she did find a job in Seattle, how long would it be before she would have to move on?

Don't think about it, she told herself. *Catch your moments of happiness while you can.*

She coiled her arms around his neck, her heart turning over with love for him. "I have to work tomorrow. But I'm free for the weekend. I could take the evening flight. Can you set up an interview for Sunday?"

He hugged her fiercely. "You bet I can."

"Two dozen?" Desiree cried with delight as Kyle placed the enormous bouquet of red roses in her arms. The modem Seattle airport terminal still bustled with activity as she stepped off the plane at ten-thirty Friday evening.

"You shouldn't spoil me like this," she added. "A dozen roses the day after we met. Now two dozen at the airport. What's it going to be next time? *Three* dozen?"

"Definitely." His arms closed around her, sandwiching the flowers between them. "Every bride should carry three dozen red roses in her bridal bouquet."

She smiled against his lips. "Don't go jumping to conclusions, Mr. Harrison. I agreed to meet you for the weekend, but I *didn't* say I'd marry you."

"You will, my beautiful lady." His lips meshed with hers. "You will."

Through the plate-glass windows in the terminal, Desiree caught a glimpse of tall, dark evergeen trees silhouetted against the black sky. It was a refreshing change to see a city airport surrounded by pines instead of palms.

"I see you have a thing about Maseratis," she said a short time later, after Kyle had loaded her small bag in the trunk of his silver sports car and spun out onto the highway.

He nodded as he shifted the Maserati into high gear and zoomed around slower traffic. "The only way to drive. I've managed to get ahold of one of these beauties every time I've flown into L.A., but I'm not always so lucky. You should have seen the crate I got stuck with all week in Tulsa."

When he described the many problems that he'd encountered with his rented sedan, from a door that wouldn't open, to windshield wipers that wouldn't shut off, he was so comical in his delivery and so good-natured about it all that Desiree's shoulders shook and her eyes watered with helpless laughter.

A short drive took them to an elegant condominium complex in a lovely, wooded area on the outskirts of town. The Tudor-style brick-and-stucco buildings, enhanced with dark wood trim, seemed to sprout up from the depths of a dense forest.

"How beautiful." Desiree stepped out of his garage and breathed in the heady scent of the surrounding evergreens. "You'd never know we're so close to the city."

"A few more minutes down the freeway, and you're really in the countryside. You'd love it in winter. You can reach deep snow in practically no time." He unlocked the heavy, oak front door and led her inside, flipping on light switches ahead of them.

Desiree took a step down into the spacious sunken living room. Her shoes sank into the luxurious, champagne-colored carpet as she looked around her with awe. Books of every size and description and a myriad of art objects filled floor-to-ceiling teak shelves on two sides of the room, along with an elaborate stereo system, speakers, and a large television.

Colorful modern prints hung over the long, blue-grey sofa and Danish teak end tables. Track lighting illuminated the room from beams in the vaulted ceiling. There was a brick fireplace, a built-in wet bar, and a long, dark-blue tile counter that passed through into an immaculate, modern kitchen with gleaming wood cabinets.

"It's wonderful, Kyle."

He dropped her suitcase by the door, then caught her hand in his. "It is now that *you're* here. Come on. Let me show you the rest."

In addition to the living room and kitchen, the condo

boasted a study, a cheerfully decorated guest bedroom and bathroom, a large master suite, a laundry room, garage, and a small, fenced yard.

"I love it," Desiree exclaimed as Kyle rested her suitcase on a low table in a corner of the master bedroom. "But I have a confession to make. When you mentioned your house in Seattle, I never imagined a condominium. Somehow, I expected to find an enormous mansion on five acres, complete with a circular driveway and an army of servants."

"A man on his own doesn't need a big, fancy house to rattle around in. This complex was a far better investment."

"You own the whole complex?" she asked in surprise, and then laughed. "I should have guessed."

"After we're married, it'll be different. We'll build the biggest, best house that money can buy."

"We will?"

"Yes." He pulled her into his arms. "We'll get an architect to design the place to complement all your beautiful old furniture." His fingers slipped around to the buttons on the front of her blouse. "We'll get rid of my modern stuff if you want. Build a formal dining room to fit your new table."

He opened first one button, then another, punctuating the action with each word he spoke: "We'll have a music room. Game room. Two offices. Country kitchen. A giant master suite complete with sauna and Jacuzzi bathtub, built around an indoor garden."

He pulled apart the soft fabric and reached around to unsnap her bra. Then, with one hand splayed across the small of her back, he reached around with the other to cup her breast in his hand. "And five additional bedrooms. No, six."

"Six?"

"One guest room, and one room for each kid."

She gasped, as much from the effect of his nimble fingers as from his startling declaration. "Five children?"

"Well, that's negotiable." He laughed, slid his arms around her bare midriff and hugged her tightly against him. "I enjoyed growing up in a big family, and always wanted one myself." Suddenly, he drew back slightly, his voice deeply serious. "You do want children, don't you?"

"Very much. I don't know about five, but two or three at least."

He smiled. "As many as you want. And we'll hire a nanny and a cook to help take care of them while we're working."

"Sounds perfect. Almost too perfect. I think I'd be afraid of a life filled with so much ... perfection."

"We can do it, Desiree," he said softly. "Together, we can do anything."

They gazed into each other's eyes for a time, and she felt as if time had crystallized around them, sealing them in a sweet, safe vault, where happiness was guaranteed to those who loved and hoped and worked hard and dreamed the same dreams.

"I always wished I had a twin sister," she said at last. "My mother used to console me by saying I'd grow up and have twins of my own one day."

"In that case you're in luck. Twins run in my family." His eyes danced mischievously. "And I can't think of anything I'd enjoy more than making children with you."

~

"OH, NO. IT'S RAINING." Desiree looked out the bedroom window the next morning to find a light drizzle falling from a gloomy grey sky.

"A little rain won't stop us from sightseeing."

She tossed a pair of shorts and a few summer blouses onto a nearby chair as she rummaged through her suitcase for something warmer. Thank goodness she'd decided to pack jeans and a long-sleeved shirt after all. She hadn't even thought of bringing a raincoat—it was still summer.

Kyle opened his closet and pulled out a pair of jeans. "I'll make you a dollar bet it stops raining by noon."

"You're willing to risk a whole *dollar*?" she teased. "What faith."

"It's my father's favorite saying. Every time he makes a dollar bet on something he wins."

"*Every* time?" Desiree sat down on the edge of the bed to put on her sandals, then changed her mind and pulled on socks and tennis shoes instead. "This I've got to see. For a dollar, you're on."

By ten o'clock the sky had cleared to a brilliant, cloudless blue. "I told you," Kyle grinned as they hopped into his car and headed for the wharf.

"I'm a believer. I can't wait to meet your father. He sounds like a real character."

A weekend didn't leave much time for sightseeing, especially with a family dinner to attend that night and an interview at KXTR the next afternoon, but Kyle seemed determined to squeeze in as many sights as possible in the time allowed.

"Seattle was the last stop for prospectors rushing north to the Klondike in the gold rush of 1898," he explained as they walked hand in hand through the shops at Pier 70, a nineteenth century wooden steamship pier.

They climbed the steep pedestrian staircase to Pike Place Market, a noisy, colorful profusion of sidewalk stalls overflowing with country produce, flowers, and seafood, then walked back down to the waterfront on Alaskan Way.

While Kyle waited for their take-out lunch of shrimp and clams, Desiree ducked inside a shop and ordered a bright green T-shirt for Kyle stamped with the slogan, THIS SHIRT IS GREEN.

"I'll get you for this," he laughed when she presented him with the gift. When they reached the water's edge, he exacted his punishment by drawing her close against his chest and kissing her.

"Take that," he said. "And that. And that."

Despite the public place, despite the streaming fries and seafood growing cold on a nearby bench, the kissing continued for quite some time.

Desiree loved the city. She loved the blending of old and new, and the rustic waterfront and charming curiosity shops against the backdrop of modern skyscrapers just blocks away.

She loved the crisp, clean air and the tall evergreens sprouting here and there and the blue, blue sky, more vivid and clear than any sky she'd ever seen. She was fascinated by the native Indian and Eskimo crafts, the folklore and totem poles, the nearness to Alaska, and the woodsy, care-free atmosphere that seemed to pervade the area.

At a curio shop, she bought an Eskimo rock carving of

a bear devouring a wiggling fish. "It's a symbol of strength and power," she explained as they made their way back to the car. "Perfect for your desk at the office. Which, by the way, is the sight I'd like to see next."

"Which office? The one at Harrison Engineering in Auburn? Standard Tool and Die in Tacoma? Sparkle Light in St. Louis? Or maybe you'd rather see—"

"Stop showing off! I want to see your main office, in downtown Seattle."

A few minutes drive along city streets brought them to the tall, high-rise building that housed Harrison Industries headquarters on its top floor.

"I've only got a handful of people here to help keep an eye on things," Kyle explained as he gave her a swift tour of the simple suite of offices. Like his condominium, the furnishings and decor were modern and tasteful, a cheerful splash of color against stark white walls.

"The important part of this corporation are the individual companies themselves. They only consult me for an occasional problem or an important negotiation. Mainly, I sit up here and run interference."

"What a view," Desiree remarked breathlessly as he led her into his office, a large airy room with a solid wall of windows overlooking the downtown area and Elliot Bay beyond.

She stopped beside his wide desk, which was ringed with framed photographs of numerous grinning babies, grade school children, and five stunning young women. "Who are *they?*" she asked, indicating the women's pictures with a nod of her head.

"The kids? My nieces and nephews. Or were you refer-ring to all these gorgeous, sexy women?"

She cast him a shrewd look filled with mock suspicion. "Well? Who are they?"

"Jealous?" His arms came around from behind her and he pulled her back against him, adding in a low voice, "They're my sisters."

"I figured."

His voice became husky. "Mmmm. You can't imagine how many times I've imagined making love to you right here, in my office." He nuzzled her neck. "How about if I lock the door and we make one of *my* fantasies come true?"

"I wish we could," she replied softly, reluctantly, "but your parents are expecting us for dinner at six. And we have to go back to your place and change."

"Oh, that's right."

To her surprise she felt his body stiffen suddenly. His arm flashed out and grabbed a note that lay beside his phone.

"This must have come in after I left last night." He stepped aside, picked up the phone, and rapidly punched a series of numbers. "I'll just be a minute."

Desiree moved to the windows to drink in the view while he conducted his phone conversation.

"Rand?" she heard Kyle say behind her. "What time did you get in? How'd things go?"

The sun gleamed on the windows of the city buildings below, which stretched out toward a sparkling blue bay. Wouldn't I love to have a view like this every day, she thought, instead of the bleak, beige walls of my studio.

"What?" Kyle cried. "You gave up our entire negotiating position! We can't break even on the contract now."

Desiree glanced at Kyle in alarm. He was leaning against the desk, tensely gripping the phone.

"You knew where to call me. I was back in the office yesterday at noon. Dammit, you gave the thing away." He sighed, made a few more curt observations, and then hung up the phone. "Let's get out of here," he muttered in her direction, before wheeling toward the door.

Desiree followed, her stomach knotting with anxiety. What had happened? Kyle barely spoke as they rode down the elevator and drove back to his condo. When he'd unlocked the front door and ushered her inside, he finally told her what was wrong.

"Because I left Tulsa early," he said, crossing the living room and heading down the hall, "Standard Tool and Die just lost a hundred thousand dollars."

She gasped. "A hundred thousand dollars! Why?"

Kyle stopped in the doorway of his bedroom and faced her. "The client put the pressure on while I was gone. My negotiator panicked. He lowered the price and gave away all our potential profit on the contract."

"Oh, Kyle. I'm so sorry." She reached out to touch him with a sympathetic gesture, but he responded with a deprecating wave of his hand.

"It's not the money. It's the *principle* of the thing. Two hundred people will be busting their butts to meet a deadline, and for what? We won't make a dime. We don't need busy work. What a waste." Shaking his head, he strode into the bedroom. "If I had just stayed and finished the job myself ...."

He stumbled, then bent down to pick up something from the floor. A white leather sandal. Her sandal. He whirled on her, holding the shoe aloft. "And by the way, put your stuff away, would you? You've been here less than twenty-four hours and already the place is a mess. I could have killed myself on these." He picked up the offending sandal's mate and tossed them both in a corner.

"Sorry."

A wave of guilt washed over her. He was right—she shouldn't have left her shoes out like that. She felt horrible that he'd tripped because of her. But as her eyes darted around the room, the only other evidence of her misbehavior was a few items of her clothing that lay on the bed and on a nearby chair, and a glass of water on the nightstand.

"I'm sorry, too, if I'm not neat enough for you," she added, her voice clear and even. "I agree, my things aren't in perfect order, but I'd hardly call it a mess."

He just frowned in response. "We've got fifteen minutes to get dressed. I'm going to take a shower. Join me if you want."

"No thank you," she returned.

He disappeared into the bathroom and slammed the door.

Desiree sank down onto the bed, heart pounding in dismay. Could this really be the same bed where they had made slow, luxurious love that very morning? Could this be the same man who'd held her so tenderly in his arms and whispered words of love?

She knew his anger stemmed not from a misplaced shoe or some scattered clothing, but from the news of his negotiation gone wrong. And that was what hurt the most.

If he hadn't left Tulsa a day early to see her, he'd have finished the negotiations himself … and, no doubt, would have gotten the client to give up every penny of that hundred thousand dollars, and more.

Because she'd made him feel guilty for breaking their date the previous weekend, he'd ignored his obligations and had flown down to L.A. to see her. If anyone was to blame for his company's loss, it was probably she.

She'd told Kyle that a long-distance relationship would be fraught with problems. And she'd been right. Still, she hadn't expected anything so serious or so costly to happen, or so soon. Already she felt as if she'd become a major thorn in his side.

With a heavy sigh, she unbuttoned her blouse, then folded it and the other clothes she'd left out and replaced them in her suitcase. Taking her outfit for the evening out of Kyle's closet, she clutched the hangers to her chest.

What timing, she thought. A family dinner. She had to go; it would be rude to back out at this point. But Kyle was so upset. How on earth would she get through it?

CHAPTER 12

"**Y**ou said this was going to be a small family dinner."

"It is. Just a few close relatives."

They'd finished dressing with a minimum of conversation and driven to a quiet residential area on the north side of town. Kyle parked at the curb near a charming, two-story, red-brick house, and helped Desiree out of the car. She counted seven other vehicles crowding the curb and driveway.

"How many relatives is a few?"

"It would be more," Kyle said in a clipped tone as he headed briskly up the curving, red-brick walkway, "but my oldest sister and her four kids moved to Des Moines last year."

Desiree could see that he was still irritated, a mood that threw a gloomy cloud over everything. She pressed her lips together. She'd be damned if she'd let it affect her. She was here to meet his family. She'd have a good time if it killed her.

She turned her attention to the heady fragrance of the rose bushes blooming vibrantly on either side of the path. Neat hedges and colorful flower beds surrounded a verdant, green lawn, and she noticed a long wooden swing, similar to the one she had at home, hanging from the porch rafters.

The front door stood open behind an aging screen door, and she could hear laughing voices and bustling activity inside.

She readjusted the delicate combs that pulled her hair back on either side of her face. They were handmade and covered with tiny seashells. It seemed hard to believe that Kyle had just bought them for her on their carefree expedition that afternoon.

The fluted neckline of her midnight-blue blouse was embroidered in the same color with flowers in a cut-away design, and she wore steel-grey slacks with matching pumps. She'd packed the outfit with such high hopes, wanting to make a good impression on Kyle's parents.

"Do I look all right?" she asked.

Kyle stepped up onto the porch without a backward glance. "You look fine."

"How would you know?" Desiree scoffed. "You haven't looked at me once since you stepped out of the shower."

He turned and shot a glance in her direction. A pause followed, in which his expression changed, softening with what appeared to be newfound awareness laced with guilt. He opened his mouth to speak, but just then a young voice called out:

"Kyle's here!" A boy stared out at them from behind the

screen door, then darted away. "Mom! Kyle's here with his girlfriend!"

Before they could move, a petite, attractive brunette pushed open the screen door. Desiree recognized her from one of the pictures on Kyle's desk.

"Hey! We were starting to think you two had skipped town on us." The young woman stepped out and squeezed Desiree's hands warmly. "It's Desiree, right? I'm so glad to meet you. I'm Linda, Kyle's sister." Desiree couldn't help returning the woman's friendly smile.

Linda turned and gave her brother a big hug. "It's about time you brought someone home to meet the family. Mom's in a positive tizzy. She's been cooking all day. Now come on in," she told Desiree. "Everyone's dying to meet you."

Desiree took a deep breath as she walked inside. She'd done her best to avoid crowds and promotional events during her radio career. And her childhood, spent in a rambling house with only one brother and a pair of reclusive parents, had in no way prepared her for the hubbub of a big family gathering.

And a big family gathering it was. In quick succession she was introduced to three more friendly sisters, two brothers-in-law with hearty handshakes, more than half a dozen giggling and gurgling nieces and nephews, an elderly aunt, a bachelor uncle, two Siamese cats, and a bouncing golden retriever.

One of the brothers-in-law pounded Kyle on the back. "Way to go, buddy," he said, winking in Desiree's direction.

To her surprise, Desiree found herself responding almost immediately to their infectious enthusiasm.

Everyone seemed delighted to meet her and strove to make her feel welcome. Soon she was laughing, matching quip with quip, and bantering as freely as she did on the air.

"Pay close attention, now," teased Kelli Ann, an attractive woman in her mid-twenties. "There'll be a quiz on names and birth dates after dinner."

"I'll never pass!" Desiree laughed.

She chatted with Kelli for a while, and learned she was a graphic designer who worked in advertising. They were both passionate about their work. Desiree felt that she'd met a kindred spirit.

"By the way, Kyle," Kelli remarked, "I thought of a new slogan for that diet soft drink of yours."

"Oh yeah?" Kyle responded. "What's that?"

Kelli raised one hand, and as if writing in the air, said, "Sparkle Light: One Awesome Calorie."

Kyle took that in. "Not bad, Kelli."

"Not bad?" Desiree echoed. "I think it's brilliant. You should hire her."

Kelli laughed. "I like this woman."

For the first time since they'd arrived, Desiree caught Kyle's eye. A flicker of deep emotion crossed his face, something like admiration mingled with sincere regret.

She felt a stirring within her, and she smiled hesitantly, hopefully. He started to take a step toward her when a cheerful voice rang out above the party hum:

"There you are!" A rosy-cheeked wisp of a woman in a purple dress and plaid apron squeezed through the crowd and laid a hand on Desiree's shoulder. Her short, dark-brown hair was streaked with grey, and the laugh lines around her mouth and pale-blue eyes promised a sunny personality. "I'm Stephanie, Kyle's mother. I'm so delighted you could come."

Desiree knew at once that she would like her. As she thanked Stephanie for inviting her, Desiree's heart swelled with gratitude for the welcome she'd received.

Kyle leaned down and gave his mother a warm hug and a kiss. "You look beautiful tonight as always, Mom. Is that leg of lamb I smell?"

"What else would I make for my favorite son but his favorite meal?"

He chuckled. At the same time his eyes met and found Desiree's. "I'll take the compliment, even though I'm her only son."

Desiree couldn't help but smile. In his gaze, she read a silent, earnest apology and a plea for forgiveness. Her heart turned over.

No relationship, she realized, was perfect every single second. So, he'd lost his temper a while ago. She understood why. She still felt bad about her own part in making it happen. And she did forgive him.

"I'm sorry the place is such a zoo," Stephanie remarked. "I warned the girls to leave a few of the kids at home, but they all insisted on coming."

"I'm glad," Desiree replied. "In a family this size, it's better to just jump right in and meet everybody at once."

"Brave girl you've got here," Stephanie told Kyle.

Suddenly, Desiree realized that she'd love to be a part of this big, happy, exuberant family. It may never happen, but just for tonight she wanted to pretend that it could. She gave him an answering look that spoke of her love and granted him amnesty.

He heaved a sigh of relief and stepped closer, as if to take her into his arms. Before he made contact, though, a glass door slid open at the back of the room. "Hey, why didn't someone tell me they were here?"

Desiree jumped, startled. If Kyle hadn't been standing next to her, she would have sworn the voice she'd heard was his. She turned around and caught her breath.

The man crossing the room could only be Kyle's father. Except for the facial lines etched by time in this man's handsome face and the silvery hair threaded thickly among the brown, the resemblance between the two was uncanny.

He possessed Kyle's trim powerful build, the same brilliant green eyes, the same high cheekbones and gracefully angled nose. She felt as if she'd been granted a vision of how youthful and attractive Kyle would still appear in years to come.

"Well, well. Hello and welcome," he said, enfolding Desiree's hand in both of his. "I'm Dan, the old man of the house."

"Old man, nothing!" Desiree heard herself say. Laughter shouted out around her.

"I knew I was going to like her." Dan grinned. "Say, has anybody given you a tour of this place yet? No? Well then, come on."

She flashed Kyle an apologetic glance as she was led away. He hid a smile and telegraphed a return message of frustrated longing.

A small crowd of youngsters tagged along behind as Dan showed Desiree around the house. She felt overwhelmed by the sense of warmth and love of family that seemed to radiate throughout.

Pictures of Kyle, his sisters, and the grandchildren hung everywhere, together with framed awards and countless childish but clearly cherished attempts at pottery, weaving, watercolor, and finger painting. The children proudly pointed out their own particular works of art, and Desiree praised their efforts.

Dan had an amusing anecdote for nearly all of the rooms, which were stuffed with odds and ends of furniture, some new, some old, as if he and his wife couldn't bear to throw anything out. The general clutter made her feel right at home. *At least his parents aren't neat freaks,* she thought with a smile.

"Soup's on!" Stephanie cried. Dan led her back to the dining room and rang a loud brass gong hanging beside the kitchen door. The children scrambled out to the back porch, where a picnic table had been set for them.

An arm darted out from the general uproar, and to her delight, Desiree found herself nestled in Kyle's arms, against his chest.

"I think there's something to be said for small families after all," he growled. "Whose idea was it to come here, anyway?"

She tipped her head back and smiled at the affection reflected in his eyes. "Yours," she said. "And it was one of your better ideas. I love your family."

He kissed her, long and hard. Around them she heard good-natured hoots and catcalls.

"Hey, cut out the mushy stuff!" a voice cried.

"Save it for Christmas, under the mistletoe!"

They pulled apart, laughing.

Desiree took a seat next to Kyle at one end of the long

dining-room table. Throughout the delicious meal, she was besieged with friendly questions about herself and her work. She heard countless Harrison family stories and shot back with a few tales of her own, which were met with uproarious and appreciative laughter.

"Kyle offered to buy us a big, new house after he started doing so well," Stephanie confided, leaning across the table toward Desiree. "And you know what I said? I said, thank you, but no thank you. I raised six children in this house. It was big enough then, and it's big enough now. And if you think I'm going to pack all those pictures and knickknacks and whatnots to move somewhere else, you've got another guess coming."

"Grandpa! Grandpa! Guess what?" A small girl in pigtails raced into the room and climbed onto her grandfather's lap. "I passed the Polliwog test at swim lessons and next week I'll be a Frog!"

"Wonderful, sweetheart." Daniel kissed the freckled cheek. "Keep up the good work. Maybe you'll make the high school swim team someday."

"High school, nothing," said the girl's father. "Someday she'll make the Olympic swim team."

Daniel slapped the tabletop. "Damn right! Excuse me, Stephanie. Say, who wants to make a dollar bet Tracy makes it to the Olympics?" Wallets flashed and several dollar bills were flung on the table amid general laughter and applause.

"You wait and see," Kyle told Desiree with a knowing wink. "She'll make it."

By the time the peach and apricot pies were brought out for dessert, Desiree felt as if she'd been a part of this fun-loving family for years. After coffee, adults and children alike spilled out onto the front driveway, where Kyle's father pulled out a box of fireworks left from the family Fourth of July party.

The children raced around the yard, drawing designs in the darkness with blazing sparklers. Everyone clapped in delight as screaming rockets sailed through the air and fire fountains gushed red, white, and blue up to the night sky. Caught up in the excitement of the celebration, Desiree waved sparklers and shouted her delight along with the rest of them.

All too soon, the evening came to an end. Dishes were done, goodbyes said, and families piled into individual cars for the drive home.

"I hope we'll be seeing you again soon, and often," Stephanie said as she hugged Desiree goodbye on the front porch.

"You will, Mom." Kyle wrapped his arms around Desiree.

"Who wants to make a dollar bet we dance at their wedding before the year's over?" Daniel asked, a twinkle in his eye.

"It's a bet." Kyle whipped a dollar out of his pocket and shook his father's hand with gusto.

A warm glow started in the pit of Desiree's stomach and spread to the tips of her fingers and toes. *Every time my dad makes a dollar bet, he wins,* Kyle had said.

If things worked out at the radio station tomorrow, if they offered her a job, maybe, just maybe ....

"Have a good time?" Kyle asked a few minutes later,

after they'd climbed into his car and were speeding down the highway.

"I had a great time. Your family's wonderful. Every one of them."

"Ah! But then you haven't met my cross-eyed Aunt Bernice from Boston, who lives in an attic, has twenty-seven cats, and paints moody abstracts of dancing flamingos in tutus."

"Sounds to me like she'd fit right in."

They laughed. "Hey, woman, come here." He extended one arm across her shoulders, gently pulling her against him as he drove with his left hand. "I've been dying for a moment alone with you all night. I wanted to apologize for acting like a complete jerk this afternoon."

"Apology accepted. But I understand why you were angry. A hundred-thousand-dollar loss is no laughing matter. I feel so bad. It's my fault that you left Tulsa early, and my fault that I—"

"None of it was your fault. Leaving early was my own decision, and I had no right to take out my frustration on you. Harrison Industries isn't going to collapse over one lousy contract. And Kyle Harrison won't collapse if a few shoes are strewn around his bedroom."

"Are you sure?"

"I'm sure." He kissed the top of her head and massaged her neck beneath her mane of hair. "I love you, Desiree, and I love everything about you."

"Good to know." She smiled and leaned her head against his shoulder. "Because I love you back."

◊

"YOUR SKIN IS SO SOFT. I love the way you feel."

They were inside the glass-enclosed shower at Kyle's condo, where his soapy hands traveled across Desiree's shoulders, over her breasts, and down the sleek incline of her waist.

"I love the way *you* feel," she replied, running her fingers over his slippery, wet biceps.

She grabbed the bar of scented soap and stood on tiptoe to wash Kyle's shoulders and lather the hair across his chest. Her massaging fingers followed the bubbles which slid down the V-shaped wedge of hair and then further down, past his navel.

"Be careful what you touch down there," he cautioned, taking a sharp breath, "unless you want to be dragged out of this shower and into the bedroom before we get a chance to rinse off."

"You wouldn't." Her eyes flashed a teasing challenge as she pulled him against her. She rubbed soap across the small of his back, down his buttocks, to the back of his thighs. "Think of the messy trail of hot, soapy water we'd leave across the floor all the way to the bed."

"Yes. Think of it." He grabbed her around the waist and reached for the shower door handle, but she wriggled out of his grasp and jumped back under the shower's warm spray.

"Stop!" She raised her fists in a fighter's stance and glared at him. Water ricocheted off her head and shoulders in a fine spray and soapy rivulets drifted down her chest and abdomen. "I'm not leaving this shower until I'm finished."

He laughed, then took the bar of soap from her and

built up a frothy lather in his hands. "All right. I concede. As long as I'm allowed the honors of finishing."

He crouched down before her and began to soap her calves with long, loving strokes. She didn't protest. When his soapy fingers reached up to tantalize her thighs, and then, with gentle massaging motions, moved ever closer to her womanhood, a small moan escaped her lips and she was obliged to grasp his shoulders for support.

Sliding his arms around her waist, he kissed his way up over her stomach, finally pausing to sip the warm water streaming down the narrow valley between her breasts.

"You're one beautiful woman, Desiree." He ran his tongue around the lower perimeter of one breast, then up to flick back and forth across its crest.

Her fingers twined in his wet hair, pulling him still closer against her. "Do you have any idea ... what that does to me?"

In answer, he straightened to his full height and pressed her mouth to his. She could feel his desire pinned between them. "The same thing it does to me, my love," he said thickly.

Taking a ragged breath, he leaned back against the shower wall, worshiping the length of her body with his eyes, reaffirming how much he loved every plane and hollow and curve.

A flame kindled deep within her and her eyes brimmed over in response. Taking her in his arms, he sat down on the tile seat, pulling her onto his lap.

"Kyle ....?" she said, more with surprise than hesitation as he held her suspended in his embrace, propped on the tile seat.

"You said," he intoned teasingly, "that you wouldn't leave until you were finished."

"I did."

"Well, then. Let's *finish*."

She nodded her assent. She was ready, more than ready, and she lowered herself onto him, sheathing him with her loving warmth. His fingers dug into the firm flesh of her thighs as he sealed his mouth to hers.

She could feel the tension building within him, a mirror of her own rising passion. Their tongues moved in an erotic mating dance, keeping pace with the movement of their bodies. Heat pulsed through her veins, a fire that couldn't be quenched by the water spraying against their fevered skin.

They rocked, bodies fused together, with a rhythm as ageless as the sea. And then, together, they hurtled off the edge of the earth.

MUCH LATER, they lay in bed facing each other, heads cushioned by the same pillow, arms and legs entwined in the darkness. His fingers toyed gently with damp strands of her hair.

"Marry me, Desiree," he said softly.

"I want to, Kyle," she whispered. "You know that. But even if I manage to get a job in Seattle, even if everything works out the way we want ... can you really put up with someone like me forever? I'm not the neatest person in the world, and I don't know if I can change."

"I don't expect you to change for me." Lovingly, he

stroked the curve of her neck. "I was so proud to be with you tonight. My family adored you, just as I knew they would."

She snuggled up against him, resting her head on his shoulder as she sighed. "I wish you could meet my family. They'd love you, too. But my brother's in Denver now. My parents moved to Florida after they retired. I can't take any more time off, and to get any of them to come out west before Christmas would take an act of God."

"Or a wedding."

She looked up to meet his gaze through the darkness. The hunger she saw there caused her heart to pump wildly.

"Or a wedding," she echoed softly.

CHAPTER 13

"It's breathtaking."

Despite foreboding weather, Desiree and Kyle had spent the morning touring the Pacific Science Center, and decided to have lunch at the elegant, revolving restaurant atop the 605-foot Space Needle.

They now sat at a small window table, admiring the panoramic view of the city and surrounding lakes, bays, and mountains, marred only by the gathering dark clouds that seemed to be closing in on them with astonishing speed.

"We've got about an hour of sunshine before it starts to rain," Kyle responded, with the certainty of a man who's lived in a rainy climate all his life. "Since the restaurant makes one full rotation every hour, you'll get to see the whole view by then."

Their spinach salads and fresh broiled salmon were scrumptious. They agreed to skip dessert, admitting that they'd both splurged far too often on sinfully fattening foods over the past few weeks.

Just as they emerged below from the high-speed elevator, the sky opened up. They raced back to the car, huddling together under Kyle's umbrella. Despite the overhead protection, huge drops splashed against Desiree's open-toed shoes and seeped through her stockings to drizzle down her legs.

"Wow!" She slammed the car door and slumped against her seat. "When it rains here, it really rains."

"You ain't seen nothing yet. This storm is just getting started." Kyle pulled out from the curb, adding, "I like the rain. I like the sound of it on the roof and the smell of it in the air."

"I like rain, too ... if I'm inside looking out. And splashing through puddles on a rainy day can be fun." The windshield wipers were fighting a losing battle against the steadily increasing torrent.

Desiree shook out the skirt of her burgundy dress, which was covered in visible wet spots. Glancing in the vanity mirror on the visor, she cringed at the wayward tendrils of hair around her face which had frizzed in the moist air. "But I don't like to get soaked right before a job interview."

"Don't worry. They expect you to be a little soggy around here. Everyone's used to it."

A few minutes later, he parked in front of a tall, high-rise building in the center of town, then gave her directions to find the radio station.

"Ed Alder and the receptionist came in especially for this appointment. They said the door would be unlocked. I'll wait for you down here." He kissed her. "Good luck, sweetheart."

"Thanks. And thanks again for setting this up."

She opened her umbrella against the downpour, then stepped out and hurried up the street to the building's wide, glass doors. A quick elevator ride brought her up to the top floor.

Desiree caught her breath in astonishment when she stepped into the sleek, modern lobby with its plush, red carpeting and gleaming oak furniture. The KXTR logo and slogan, *Something XTRa for Seattle,* were mounted in shiny, gold, three-dimensional letters on a mirrored wall behind the receptionist's huge desk.

This makes KICK look like it's stuck in the stone age, Desiree thought, recalling her station's black vinyl benches, ancient linoleum, and nondescript lobby decor.

She introduced herself to the receptionist, who buzzed the program director on her phone.

"Mr. Alder will see you now," the young woman said to Desiree. "Please follow me."

She led her past a glass cabinet filled with trophies and awards, down a long hall hung with framed photographs of deejays, and stepped into a room which put the offices at KICK to shame.

Textured wallpaper was printed in subtle beige with the logo pattern of the broadcasting company that owned the station. The desk, which dominated the room, was massive and modern. A bar was built into one corner. Leafy potted plants stood regally beside floor-to-ceiling windows, which offered a magnificent if rain-streaked view of the city below.

"Mr. Alder?" the receptionist said. "This is Desiree Germain."

A ruddy-faced, dark-haired man unfolded himself from a swivel chair and extended a large hand to her across the desk.

"Miss Germain. It's a pleasure to meet you." His face broke into a wide grin. He spoke with a pronounced Texas twang.

She returned his smile and firm handshake. "I'm pleased to meet *you*, Mr. Alder. Thank you for seeing me on a Sunday. I know the station runs seven days a week, but I'm sure you don't usually come in over the weekend."

"No problem, no problem at all. I understand your time constraints. You've got a job to do." His long arm swept toward the leather chair facing his desk. "Please, have a seat."

While she continued to admire the imposing office, he sat back down and told her the history of the station. She'd done her homework; she knew quite a bit about the station already, but he cited facts about its ratings and advertising rates that further impressed her.

"They stole me away from a top Houston station last year," he said proudly, "and I'm doing my damnedest to make us the highest rated station in the Pacific Northwest."

She filled him in with details of her background and experience that weren't listed on her resume. After chatting for about half an hour, he offered to take her on a tour of the place.

The station was the epitome of modern sophistication. The newsroom and sales offices were sharp and clean. Production rooms were outfitted with the latest equipment, and the music library was immense and well-organized. He led her past two small, empty control rooms, then stopped at the third door where a familiar red beacon flashed just outside.

Desiree looked through the window beside the door into the glass-paneled room. A man sat at an enormous, state-of-the-art console, moving his hands animatedly as he spoke into the mike. His deep tones emanated from speakers overhead.

She took an excited breath. The equipment was *gorgeous*. Nothing like the antiquated console she worked with at KICK. Her hands fairly itched to touch that board, to move those beautiful levers up and down.

Then her gaze fell on the binder that lay open on the counter before the deejay. Surprised, she asked: "Do you work from a script?"

"We do," Mr. Alder replied. "Only way to control what goes on the air."

Desiree bit her lip as disappointment surged through her. The stations where she'd worked in the past had always allowed her to speak extemporaneously—to ad lib and joke as she pleased. She'd never worked from a script and wasn't sure she would like it. It seemed to her that it would remove all the spontaneity and excitement from the job.

Oh, well, she reminded herself, *you can get used to anything.*

"So, what do you think?" Ed asked after they'd returned to his office and taken their former seats.

"Very nice," Desiree said sincerely. "You run a beautiful operation here."

"That we do. Now, let's get down to business. I'll be honest with you. We've only ever had one female deejay at KXTR, and she didn't work out too well. But Kyle Harrison's spent a lot of advertising dollars at this station, so I listened to the tape you sent. It was pretty good."

She waited expectantly as he sat back in his chair.

"You've got some decent experience. Your on-air personality is a real departure from what we've tried in the past. I can't be sure how you'll go over, and ratings, you know, are the name of the game. But I'm willing to take a chance on you. I'd like to offer you a position."

Desiree's heart leapt. Was it going to be that easy?

"I have to tell you up front, though," he went on, "there's no way we can match or even come close to the salary you're earning now." He named a figure that was almost insultingly low.

"Mr. Alder," she replied, frowning, "that's not much more than I earned in my first position seven years ago."

"Well, that's the best we can do. I've heard rumors about a possible buyout at KICK. You might be out of a job soon. I'm offering you a position if you want it. And after talking to Kyle—if I'm reading my signals right—salary won't really be the deciding factor here, will it?"

Desiree felt her cheeks redden. "What do you mean?"

"You two are getting hitched, right?"

"We might be," she admitted, "but—"

"Well, any wife of Kyle Harrison's won't have to work. And if she does, she sure as heck won't have to worry about the size of her paycheck, am I right?"

Striving to remain polite, Desiree asked, "Which shift would I have? Morning or afternoon?"

"We can use a voice like yours on nights."

"Nights?" If he'd slapped her in the face, she couldn't have been more stunned.

"Two A.M. to 6 A.M. Five days a week." His white teeth flashed as he added magnanimously, "With weekends off. How's that sound to you?"

"Mr. Alder, I worked evenings and nights for seven years. I have the afternoon drive at KICK now. My show receives critical acclaim. When Arbitron comes out with the new ratings, we expect it to be one of the top shows in the area."

"May be, little lady, but that's Anaheim. Doesn't surprise me if things are different down there next to Hol-ly-wood." He emphasized the three syllables of the word with mild derision. "But this is the Pacific Northwest. And let's be frank. You've got a bedroom voice. The kind men want to hear late at night."

Desiree felt the hot rush of color sweep from her cheeks to her forehead. *A bedroom voice?* She shot out of her chair, her heart pumping furiously.

"Thank you for your offer," she said calmly. "I'll certainly consider it and let you know." Before he could reply, she grabbed her purse and stalked from the room.

"WILL THIS RAIN EVER LET UP?" Desiree peeled her damp, clinging dress over her head and threw it over the shower stall in Kyle's bathroom. In her haste to leave the station, she'd forgotten her umbrella and had been drenched by the downpour.

"It should be over in a couple of hours." Kyle tossed her

a fluffy towel and she vigorously dried her wet hair. "I'm sorry I didn't warn you to bring a raincoat this weekend."

"I should have thought of it myself." She stripped off her wet underclothes, hung them up to dry, and ran the towel over her body. "I know that it rains a lot in Seattle. I guess I was hoping for blue skies in summer."

"We do get blue skies—you had a glimpse of them yesterday. And they're stunning. It's the rain that makes everything so crisp, clean, and green. Don't you get tired of all that sunshine back home?"

"Never."

"It's always the same in Southern California. No change of seasons."

"I like it that way. It's beautiful. Warm. Dry. And predictable."

He followed her into the bedroom, watching as she put on a bra, underwear, and a pair of jeans.

His eyes glimmered. "Are you sure you want to get dressed?"

"Yes. I'm cold." She drew her long-sleeved, cotton top over her head.

"I can think of another way we can get warm."

He stepped toward her, but she raised a hand to stop him. "Not now, Kyle." At his look of disappointment, she added, "I'm sorry, but I'm not in the mood. I just had the worst interview of my life."

He sat down on the edge of the bed with a frown. "I know, and *I'm* sorry. You have every right to be upset. I should have done my homework before sending you in there. Alder's offer was insulting. But it's only one station. There are others. I can call—"

"No. I'm not going through that kind of embarrassment again." She crossed to the window, where beating rain blurred the glass in thick rivulets, obscuring the distant pines. "Ed Alder made it clear that the only reason he bothered to listen to my tape or meet with me was because of his relationship with you. I want a job on my own merit, not as payment for your faithful advertising."

He winced at that but said: "I don't blame you. I was just trying to help."

"I know. And I appreciate all the effort you went to on my behalf, I really do. But I won't work for someone who doesn't respect my talent. And I refuse to take another night shift. I might get stuck in that rut again for years. You can't imagine what havoc that kind of schedule plays with your life. I won't take a step backward. I paid my dues. I won't do it again."

He nodded slowly. "In your shoes, I wouldn't either. But please, try another station. This time, I'll stay out of it."

She dropped down beside him on the bed, clasping her hands together. "Kyle, I love you. But—I don't want to try another station."

"Why not?"

"I want to stay in California."

He blew out a deep, disappointed sigh. "For how long?"

"I don't know." She stretched out sideways on the bed and absently traced the line of stitching in the blue quilted comforter with her index finger. "When you first suggested I look for a job in Seattle, I agreed to give it a try. I almost had myself convinced it would work. But I was wrong. And it's not just the rain, or the rude things Alder said about my voice. It's everything Southern California has to offer— commercials, TV, film. It's all there. I have a follow-ing, a reputation in that market. I can't leave now, just because the station *might* be sold. I'd be crazy to give up what I've worked so hard for."

He dropped down beside her, his jaw tense, his eyes riveted to hers. "You'd be crazy to give up what we have."

"I agree," she returned softly. "I'm not talking about giving up our relationship."

"You're not?"

She smiled lovingly into his eyes, touched his cheek with her hand. "I want to marry you, Kyle. But I want to stay at KICK."

His forehead furrowed. "How do you propose we do that? Live in separate cities?"

"Yes."

He cursed and looked away.

"There's no guarantee we can ever live in the same place for long, anyway. So, there's no reason why we have to start out that way, is there?"

He stood up and raked his hand through his hair. "What makes you so certain you'd have to move on, even if you did lose a job? Who says you couldn't find work at another station in the same area?"

"Because a deejay cast adrift is practically untouchable in the same market. Don't ask me why. It's the way the business works."

He strode across the room and braced his arms on the dresser top, his back to her. "So, even if we get married, we can only look forward to seeing each other on weekends and vacations? Twice a month here, twice a month in Southern California—at best?"

"Or maybe we can buy a house in the San Francisco Bay Area and meet halfway."

He whipped around to look at her. "Is that what you want?"

"*You're* the one who suggested we meet on weekends. You're the one who said a long-distance relationship could work. I'm just trying to make the best of it."

He shook his head bitterly. "That was before I tried it. I can see now why your marriage fell apart."

She stared at him. "What are you saying?"

"I'm saying … you were right. I don't think it *can* work. At least not for me. I've spent the past few weeks here in body, but not in spirit. And now my business is suffering."

She swallowed hard, knowing he was referring to the blown contract. Tears threatened and she fought hard to keep them at bay.

"I love you, Desiree. But I don't want to be torn, day after day, between you and my work. I want to be together, live in the same house, share the same bed. I want to spend mornings and evenings with you, make love to you every night, and wake up beside you every morning. I want to make a home together, raise children together. I want a full-time partner … for life."

She nodded, the sound of the rain beating against the windowpane matching the dull thudding of her heart.

"I want those things, too," she said quietly. "And I wish more than anything that we could make it happen. But I don't see how it's possible for us."

CHAPTER 14

Desiree shivered beneath her sweatshirt as she trudged barefoot across the damp sand and avoided scattered masses of dark, stringy seaweed.

An early morning fog hung low over the Santa Barbara coastline, casting a dull, white glow across the bay.

She'd walked this beach every morning for eight days now, trying to make some sense out of her life. Sam, her boss at KICK, had insisted she take the time off.

"You've been acting like a ghost all week," he'd growled, "here, but not really here. Something's eating you up inside. One of these days you're gonna break. And I like you too much to sit around and wait for that to happen."

"I'm fine," Desiree had insisted. "Really, I—"

"The hell you are. I'm giving you next week off." He'd waved away her protest with an impatient hand. "Go away somewhere. Relax. Don't tell me where you're going. And don't come back until you've solved your problem, whatever it is. Got it?"

Santa Barbara, the quiet, stately community just up the coast, had seemed the ideal place to meditate in solitude. But now, on the Monday morning she was due back at work, she had yet to make peace with herself. She'd checked out of the hotel and knew she ought to get in her car and drive home. But she didn't feel ready.

Her heart still ached, and tears came to her eyes every time she recalled the Sunday afternoon two weeks ago when she'd left Seattle.

Kyle had begged her to wait and take her scheduled flight the next morning. But there had seemed no point in staying. Every extra moment she spent with him would only make the ultimate parting even harder to bear.

"Stop packing, please," he'd said, as she threw clothes into her suitcase. "Don't walk out on me like this. Not now. It's pouring outside."

"It's better if I go now." She'd snapped her case shut with a bitter thud. "We've said all we have to say. I'll call a cab."

"Don't be ridiculous. If you're so set on leaving, I'll drive you to the airport."

"Thank you."

They'd sat in tense silence as Kyle steered the Maserati over the wet streets, rain pelting the windshield. When they finally reached the airport, he'd carried her bag to the counter, waited while she changed her reservation, then walked her to the gate. The flight was just about to board. Desiree had fumbled miserably with the shoulder strap on her purse as she avoided his gaze.

"Kyle, I want you to know how much I appreciate everything you've done for me," she'd said brokenly. "I've felt like a different person since we met. You've given me more confidence than I've ever had before. I'll always be grateful to you for that."

When she'd raised her eyes to his, the pain contorting his face had hurt her like a physical blow. She'd bit her lip against an onrush of tears. "I'm so sorry," she'd finished, her voice barely a whisper.

He had briefly taken her hand and squeezed it tightly. "So am I." Without another word, he'd turned and disappeared into the crowd.

Three days after she returned home, a small box had arrived with a card from Kyle. "Desiree: I'll always love you," the card had read. "Like the contents of this white box, we're a perfect matched pair. We belong together. There's got to be a way we can work things out. Please. Come back to me."

A wistful ache had wrenched at her heart, not just from the words on the card, but from the box itself.

It was pink, not white. Inside, on a bed of pale pink velvet, rested a set of custom-crafted pierced earrings: two delicate golden songbirds, similar to her pendant, with a sparkling diamond chip in each eye.

She'd burst into tears.

The earrings were still in the box, buried under the scarves in her bottom dresser drawer. Would she ever be able to bring herself to wear them?

The squawk of a seagull yanked Desiree back to the present. She blinked back fresh tears, curling her toes into the damp sand as she walked. She remembered another sea gull's cry on an idyllic afternoon with Kyle on Catalina Island.

Years, not weeks, seemed to have passed since that wonderful day. The pain of loneliness and loss spread throughout her body until her insides felt like one immense, gaping chasm.

Try to remember what life was like before you met him, she told herself, as she trudged up the sand and across the parking lot to her car. Were you happy? Did you look forward to each new day? *Yes!* You were lonely, but you'd learned to accept it. *And you'll learn to accept it again.*

She opened the car door, cleaned off her feet, and got in. Turning the key to auxiliary power, she flipped on the car radio.

"Hope you're having a great morning out there, Santa Barbara," said a cheerful masculine radio voice. "I sure am. On my way in this morning—"

She tuned out the voice, crossing her arms on the steering wheel as she wearily lowered her head. Radio. That's where the excitement was. The drama, the thrill, the power she wielded within the confines of her small control room. She'd always loved it. It had been her whole life.

Why, then, didn't she care as much about it anymore? Where had the magic gone?

"And now for some Streisand," said the radio voice. A pause. And then sweet, familiar notes rent the air. Desiree's head flew up and she stared at the radio as if it possessed satanic powers. "Songbird." Of all the songs to play ....

She leaned her head back against the seat and closed her eyes. She knew every note, every word. The lyrics wove through her mind and body, reaching down to her soul.

The songbird's sweet music brings others joy, the

words said. Her song sets people free. Yet no one knows the songbird. She's sad and alone ... and lonely. Who will sing for her?

Desiree's chest constricted with an ache of longing and emptiness. *I'm nothing more than a voice coming out of a box*, she realized with sudden, agonizing clarity. I make others happy. *But I'm alone. No one sings for me.*

You fool, a voice cried within her. *He* loves you. He's the music in your soul, the one who can set you free.

His words on their last day together echoed in her mind, infiltrating her very soul:

I love you, Desiree ... I want to be together, live in the same house, share the same bed. I want to spend mornings and evenings with you, make love to you every night, and wake up beside you every morning. I want to make a home together, raise children together. I want a full-time partner ... for life.

She gripped the steering wheel with fierce determination. How could she have been so blind? She wanted all the same things. And she wanted them with Kyle.

How could she have imagined that she could live without him? *She loved him.* She needed him. Her work meant nothing if she couldn't have him.

Everything will work out if only you're together, she told herself. Nothing else matters. *Nothing.*

Desiree turned on the ignition and stamped on the gas pedal. The engine roared to life. She sped out of the parking lot, down the street, and pulled to a screeching halt in front of the first phone booth she could find.

I only hope I'm not too late, she thought desperately as she jumped out of the car and raced to the phone. Dipping into her purse, she grabbed her address book and searched for Kyle's office number.

I'll find a job in Seattle, take whatever I can get, she decided. Who cares what shift it is? Who cares what I'm leaving behind? At least we'll be together.

She drummed her fingernails against the booth's glass door as she waited for the operator to put through the credit card call. She'd do her best, she reasoned, make a name for herself, and eventually, she'd be on top again.

If she lost her job some day and couldn't find another one in Seattle ... to hell with it! She'd do something else.

She didn't know what else she would do, couldn't think that far ahead. She only knew that she loved Kyle and wanted to spend the rest of her life with him. If that meant pursuing a different career, fine, she'd cross that bridge if she came it.

"Harrison Industries," an efficient female voice said on the other end of the line.

"Kyle Harrison, please." Her voice sounded unnaturally high and shrill in her ears.

"I'm sorry, Mr. Harrison is out of town. Would you care to leave a message?"

Out of town? Where was he? "Well, I ... this is Desiree Germain, and—"

"Oh, yes, Miss Germain," the woman replied cordially, as if they were old friends. "How may I help you?"

"I have to talk to him. It's important. Can you tell me where I can reach him?"

"Certainly. He's in Southern California."

Desiree gave a gasp of surprise and delight. "Can you give me the name and number of his hotel?" She scribbled down the information on a small notepad in her purse, said a hurried goodbye, and hung up.

The hotel was in Anaheim. What was he doing there? she wondered. Did he come down to see her? What would he do when he found her gone?

She called the hotel and asked for his room. She let the phone ring a good twenty times before she hung up and glanced at her watch. Nine-fifteen. Damn. Where could he be?

She jumped back into her car and roared off. Thank God she'd missed the morning rush-hour traffic. She could be home in a little more than two hours if she sped all the way, kept her eye on the rearview mirror, and didn't come into contact with any highway patrolmen.

Kyle might have stopped at the radio station and learned that she was returning to work today. If so, was there a chance that he went to her house? Please, please, wait for me my darling, she prayed silently. I'm coming back to you.

The drive seemed interminable. The car shot past long stretches of dry, arid landscape, sped through the San Fernando Valley, over the mountainous Sepulveda Pass, and past the L.A. airport, on toward Orange County.

At last, she turned onto her street, her heart pounding like a locomotive, her eyes searching for another rented Maserati.

The driveway and curb stood empty.

Maybe he came in a taxi, she thought frantically. Maybe he used his key and is waiting inside. She pulled to a halt, raced up to the front door, unlocked it, and called his name.

The house was hot and musty, as empty as the day she left it.

"Where are you, Kyle Harrison?" she shouted. Her voice echoed in the stillness.

She called the hotel again. No answer. She called his office in Seattle. "Sorry to bother you again, but I can't seem to reach Mr. Harrison at his hotel. Do you have any idea where else he might be?"

"He just left word that we could reach him at the radio station, KICK. He—"

"Oh! Of course! Thank you." Desiree hung up, elated. Since he hadn't found her at home, of course he'd go to the station! She peeled off her clothes and took a fast, hot shower.

Forty-five minutes later, she pulled into the parking lot behind the station, dressed in a denim skirt and cotton top. She pushed open the double glass doors, disappointment surging through her when she saw the deserted lobby. Only Barbara was in the room, speaking rapidly into the phone behind the reception counter.

"Yes, sir. Fine. I will." Barbara caught Desiree's eye and gestured emphatically for her to wait. "I'll put it in the mail today. Thank you for calling." She disconnected the line and stood up. "Des! At last! You're back." Her eyes gleamed with some indefinable emotion. "How was your vacation?"

"Therapeutic. Listen, has anyone been by here to see—"

"Des, big things have been happening around here while you were gone," Barbara cut in. "Westler's been in meetings all week. And guess what? He sold the station."

"Sold it? When?"

"They finalized everything yesterday. Westler took off,

but the new guy is here. He said he wants to talk with you as soon as you get in."

"Talk with me?" Desiree asked, stunned. "Why?"

"You'd better hurry. He's been waiting for ages." She shooed Desiree off toward the door that led into the station. "Go. He's in Westler's old office."

Frowning, Desiree opened the door and hurried down the hall. What was the new guy going to do? Fire her? If so, she didn't care. She intended to leave anyway.

The door to Westler's office stood open. She stepped over the threshold, then stopped, frozen. The man behind the desk looked up from a stack of papers, his handsome face unreadable, his green eyes wary.

"Hello, Desiree," Kyle said quietly.

Her mouth flew open, but no words came out. What was he doing, sitting behind Westler's desk? Was this some kind of a joke? Then suddenly, all the jumbled pieces of information she'd learned this morning fell into place in her mind like a reassembled jigsaw puzzle. She gasped in astonishment.

"You bought the radio station?"

"Yes. Would you close the door, please?"

She complied mechanically. He gestured toward the chair facing his desk. "Have a seat."

Desiree dropped stiffly into the chair, her mind whirling, alternately accepting and rejecting what she'd just heard. Kyle's eyes seemed to search hers for a sign, an indication of her feelings. But she was so taken aback she could only return his stare blankly.

He made a notation on the page in his hand, then set it

aside. "I hope you enjoyed your vacation?" His tone was calm, polite.

"It was ... fine."

"Good." He lifted several sheets from a folder and extended them to her across the desk. She didn't look at them, her eyes still focused on his face. He seemed to be struggling to maintain a businesslike façade, to keep his emotions in check.

"It'll take a few weeks before the sale is final," he said. "But in the meantime, you'll be glad to know your future at KICK is secure. You can take over as general manager, or keep your spot on the air, or both—whatever you like. I've had papers drawn up to make you a partner in the firm. You'll want to get an attorney to look them over, but what it boils down to is a fifty-percent share after five years if the company shows a consistent profit."

If she felt astonishment before, now she was completely stunned. "Fifty percent share?"

He nodded with a brief smile that ended before it reached his eyes. "Yes. You won't have to worry about job security now. Of course, you'll have a few more responsibilities, but nothing you can't handle. Does that sound okay to you? All of this is subject to your approval, obviously?"

Tears burned behind her eyes. How could he have thought she'd want the *station*? My God, the idea had never even entered her mind. She didn't even want her job anymore. She wanted *him!*

If only she could fly into his arms, make him understand. She wanted to admit how wrong she'd been, to tell him she loved him and wanted, more than life itself, to marry him.

But he was acting so calm and impersonal. When she rejected his proposal, had that killed his feelings for her? If so, why had he done all this?

"I don't know what to say." She swallowed over the lump in her throat. "I never expected you to buy the station. I don't deserve such generosity. Really. I—"

"It wasn't generosity." He stood up abruptly. His eyes met hers across the desk. "I had the funds available. I've been looking for an alternate investment in Southern California for the past month. At the moment, this station breaks even at best. But you show outstanding devotion to your work. I'm convinced that, with the incentive of partnership, you can turn this place into a real money-maker."

His words stung. He still thought the only thing she cared about was her job. He'd never forgive her for walking out on him, for choosing her career over him.

"I ... see," she managed. "Well ... I need time to think about this. I—" Her voice broke as a sob burst from her throat. Tears streamed down her cheeks. One hand flew up to cover her eyes as she rose and turned blindly for the door.

"Dammit, Desiree!" Kyle crossed the floor with urgent strides and stopped beside her. "Are you going to walk out on me again?"

She shook her head, his face a blur through a sea of tears. "I don't want to walk out on you, Kyle. But I can't stand it when you look at me that way, as if ... I'm just some employee of yours. Like there's nothing between us."

"Nothing between us?" Unfamiliar tears shone in his

eyes. "Don't you know by now how much I love you? I'll always love you, Desiree. Good God, what more can I do to prove it?"

She sobbed with relief. "Oh, Kyle. I love you, too."

"Do you?"

"Yes! *Yes.*" She wiped the moisture her cheeks as gazed up at him. "Can I say now what I've been wanting to shout to the world all day? My career doesn't mean anything to me if I can't have you. I've been so stupid. I should have realized it sooner. Do you still want to marry me? Please say you do. Because I will. With all my heart. I tried to call you this morning in Seattle to tell you, and then at your hotel, but—"

"Say that again," he interrupted, his arms instantly tightening around her.

"I tried to call you—" she began distractedly.

"No, no. The first part." His eyes began to twinkle in a familiar way and her heart lurched with newfound hope.

"I said ... I love you. If you still want me, I'll marry you."

"I accept." Their eyes met, each asking the other for forgiveness and receiving it. Then his lips came down on hers in an impassioned kiss.

She molded herself against him, returning his kiss with unrestrained fervor, trying to pour into him all the love she'd been saving, harboring, resisting.

"Has it been as hard for you as it has been for me these past weeks?" he whispered in between kisses.

"Yes. I've never been so lonely, so miserable."

"I longed for you. I reached for you in the night, but you weren't there."

"The earrings ... they're so beautiful, Kyle. I wanted to

call, to thank you. But I couldn't. I knew if I heard your voice again, I would crumble. I could never bring myself to say goodbye."

"When you didn't call after I sent the earrings, I gave up hope. I knew, then, you were lost to me forever. I thought I'd go out of my mind." He shuddered and hugged her more tightly against him. "I bought the station not only to secure your job, but ... so I'd have an excuse to see you every now and then."

She lifted her eyes to his. "Rather drastic measures to take, don't you think, Mr. Harrison?"

"Sometimes I do impulsive things," he responded with a shrug, a phrase she recalled him uttering the first day they'd met. It was incredible to think how much had happened since then, how close they'd become.

"Thank goodness you don't have any stockholders. What if the place doesn't turn a profit?"

His mouth tilted up in the lopsided grin she'd come to love so well. "Oh, it will. With you at the helm, I'm sure we'll be the top-rated station in Orange County in no time."

She hesitated. "Kyle. Wait. What you've done, it's incredible. I don't know what to say. But I can't stay here. Not if you're in Seattle."

He started to protest, but she raised a finger to his lips. "I love my work, but I love *you* more. I want to live where you are. I'll move to Seattle, and if I don't find a job or if the job doesn't last, I don't care. I'll—"

He cut off her words by covering her mouth with his. His kiss was long and sweet, communicating his love far more expressively than words. When he drew back, his eyes danced down at her. "You don't have to move to Seattle, my darling."

"Why not?"

"Because I'll move down here to be with you."

"How can you? That's impossible. Harrison Industries is—"

"Moving to Orange County," he finished. "I own a radio station here, don't I?" He lifted her hand to his lips and planted a warm kiss on her palm. "I could have looked into buying a station in Seattle, but I saw how important it was to you to stay in Southern California. So, I took a good look at my own needs and interests.

"Hell, I've only got a suite of offices up there. I can operate anywhere, as long as I'm near an airport. It'll take a few months to complete the move, and I'll have to do a bit more traveling than before, but I'll be here most of the time. My secretary's not speaking to me, but ...." He grinned. "At least my wife will be. On a daily basis."

She tried to assimilate the impact of his words. "But ... your whole family is in Seattle. You've lived there all your life."

"High time for a change. And we'll see my family on vacations, the same as yours."

"When did you decide all this?" she asked, dazed. "Why didn't you tell me before?"

"I didn't contact Westler about the possibility until a week ago. By then, you were out of town and no one knew where to find you. He had another offer, so I was forced to make a quick decision. I went ahead, hoping you'd approve. Do you?"

"Do I?" She hugged him, her heart so filled with joy she felt it might burst. "Do I ever!"

His chuckle vibrated against her chest as he lowered his face to hers. "Are you sure you won't mind spending every day of the rest of your life with me, Mrs. Harrison?"

"Even that won't be long enough, my love," she whispered before his lips claimed hers once more.

~

"AFTER THE THUNDERSHOWERS THIS MORNING, who would have expected such a gorgeous afternoon?"

Desiree smiled into the microphone. She ran her hands lovingly over the gleaming, state-of- the-art console, which Kyle had ordered the day he took possession of the station. "We've got clear blue skies all across Orange County to welcome the first day of spring. And you've got Desiree on KICK, Anaheim."

She started a commercial break, then sat back and scribbled a To Do List for herself, one of the many efficient habits she'd picked up from Kyle in the eight months that they'd been married.

1. *Call travel agent.* Kyle's birthday was next month, and she'd planned a surprise vacation to Tahiti. His coworkers knew all about it. She couldn't wait to see the expression on his face when she picked him up at the office and whisked him off to the airport.

2. *Go over financial statement.* The station had received its highest ratings ever in Arbitron's

latest book, and they'd been able to raise their advertising rates accordingly. She'd hired an assistant manager to help with her duties but conferred with Kyle on all major business decisions. And of course, she'd kept her spot on the air. It was a hectic schedule, but the daily challenge and excitement thrilled her, and she was proud of her accomplishments.

3. *Choose paint colors.* Their new house in the hills above Newport Beach was well underway. In a few months they'd be able to move in. She couldn't stop a grin as she thought about the exciting news that she planned to tell him tonight at dinner. *A different color scheme for each bedroom,* she added to her list. All six of them.

The promo ended and she switched on the mike, then flicked the lever for traffic. "It's time to check on the traffic situation. Let's talk to our man in the skies. How are you doing up there, Dave? Are the wet streets causing motorists any problems today?"

"No major accidents, Desiree." The unexpectedly deep, resonant voice caught her off-guard and sent a paroxysm of delight spiraling through her. She hadn't heard his voice over the air since the day they met!

She knew that Kyle was licensed to operate both small aircraft and helicopters and enjoyed flying in his spare time. She'd gone up in the skies with him two more times since they'd married and was getting over her fear of flying. But she'd never expected to him to take the KICK chopper for a spin.

Would he ever tire of finding ways to surprise her?

"I see we've got Killer Kyle filling in for Deadly Dave Dawson today. Did Dave take a rain check?"

"You've got it." Kyle went ahead with the traffic report, speaking smoothly, expertly, like a seasoned radio professional, giving no clue to his true identity or his lack of experience at this particular job.

"Thanks, Kyle. I hope we'll be hearing more from you," she said when he was through, unable to disguise the pride and admiration she felt for her remarkable, fun-loving husband. "Before you sign off, though, I've got a news flash that might interest you. It just came in, hot over the wire."

"I'm all ears."

"Inside sources predict there's going to be a new little deejay at KICK in about … seven months or so." Desiree bit her lip to keep it from trembling in the silence which followed.

Finally, with a slight break in his softened, deep voice, Kyle said: "Let me be the first to congratulate you … and your husband. I'm sure he must be absolutely *delighted* with the news."

With a sudden, exultant whoop of glee, he added, "I've always said, what this station needs is some fresh young talent! Who wants to make a dollar bet it's twins?"

And as all the phone lines in her control booth began to flash, their joy and laughter vibrated over the airwaves.

Like this book?

Please leave a review for FLOATING ON AIR!

Reader reviews are so appreciated! They can be short or long, or even just a star rating. Reviews are such a big help to an author.

Thank you so much!

Join Syrie's newsletter mailing list at www.syriejames.com to receive the latest news about upcoming releases and special offers just for subscribers!

AUTHOR'S NOTE

I am a romantic at heart and am especially fond of love-at-first-sight stories, about an immediate attraction between two people that rapidly turns to love.

Maybe that's because my husband and I fell in love at first sight and were married shortly thereafter. Or maybe it's because my parents, grandparents, and great-grandparents all had similar experiences, and those marriages all stood the test of time and were very happy.

Floating on Air is a newly revised edition of my first novel, previously published under the title *Songbird*. This book is especially meaningful to me because Desiree and Kyle's whirlwind romance was inspired, in part, by the challenges of a long-distance relationship that my husband Bill and I endured when we met many years ago.

I'll never forget how devastated I was each time one of us had to get on a plane and leave. But from the moment of our first meeting, we recognized in each other our missing other half!

As I lost myself in the pages of this novel again, Desiree

and Kyle's story filled me with deep and abundant joy, bringing me back to that earlier time and place. I hope you enjoyed reading *Floating on Air* as much as I enjoyed writing it!

The '80s were such an interesting time, before cell phones and the internet changed the way we do everything. Although technology has changed since then, the fundamental tenets of human relationships have not.

We all still experience the joys of a new relationship. We all still feel a deep ache in our hearts when we're separated from the ones we love. We all have made sacrifices to be together. And we all risk our hearts on the road to happiness. These things are timeless.

Loving another person … it's the grandest journey we can take … and it's what life's all about, isn't it?

It's just
business.

Or madness.

two week
DEAL

A STRUCK BY LOVE
NOVEL

USA TODAY BESTSELLING AUTHOR

SYRIE JAMES

Read on for an excerpt from

Book 2 in the

STRUCK BY LOVE SERIES:

TWO WEEK DEAL

by Syrie James

TWO WEEK DEAL - EXCERPT

CHAPTER ONE

South Lake Tahoe, California
December 1987

THE SLOT MACHINE WHIRRED. Three bright streaks of red, blue, and orange whizzed past. Kelli took a sharp breath and held it, watching as the first cylinder dropped into place with a clang: an orange on the top row, a plum in the center, cherries below. Three chances to win.

A split second later came another clang. Another plum in the center. The third cylinder continued its mad spin. Could it be? Another plum? Three plums and she'd win—

A cluster of red cherries popped into the slot next to the plums. The slot machine froze into metallic stillness.

Kelli sighed. No wonder they called it a one-armed bandit. In five seconds, she'd lost a third of tomorrow's lunch money.

Oh well, she thought with a shrug. Fortunes like mine come and go. She didn't drive all the way from Seattle to South Lake Tahoe to gamble, anyway.

She came to watch over her brother Kyle's vacation home in its last three weeks of construction and to get in some skiing—a few days of glorious downhill on some of Lake Tahoe's finest slopes. And of course, there was the job interview in San Francisco.

Kelli slid up onto the stool next to the slot machine and straightened the calf-length skirt of her white silk evening dress. Last summer, she thought with amusement, if someone had told her she'd be sitting in a casino lobby on a Friday night in early December, waiting for a man she barely knew—a man who might be her next employer—to escort her to an exclusive holiday mixer on the hotel's top floor, she wouldn't have believed it.

If she hadn't acted so impulsively, hadn't let her temper get the best of her, she'd still be working away at the ad agency in Seattle. But in the past year she'd experienced a rash of compulsions to do the boldest, most brazen things. Like the time she accepted Kyle's dare and took over the controls of his twin-engine Bonanza over Puget Sound. Crazy!

And the morning, six months ago, when she asked Wayne to pack up his things and move out, then told her boss of four years to go fly a kite and stormed out the office door without a backward glance. Madness! Her actions had shocked everyone ... including herself.

It was only later, in the ensuing weeks on her own, that she'd come to understand her motivation. For twenty-eight years she'd allowed well-meaning parents and sisters and then a domineering boyfriend to influence her every move.

Afraid of losing her job, she'd kept silent while higher-ups stole her best design work and claimed it as their own. All the while her resentment had simmered, until finally she'd blown her stack.

Life, she'd come to realize—like the ad slogan she'd helped to create—is *not* a spectator sport. Never again would she calmly sit back, letting people manipulate and take advantage of her. She was going to be in the driver's seat from now on.

She hadn't wasted any time getting her new life in order. Out from under Wayne's judgmental eye, she felt more capable, more attractive.

She had a slender figure, a face that men seemed to notice, and stick-straight reddish-brown hair that her hair-dresser envied. The world was overflowing with limitless, exciting possibilities, and she was going to enjoy every minute of it.

She had immediately indulged herself in all the things Wayne would have disapproved of. She bought clothes that were beautiful, not practical, ate take-out Chinese food five nights in a row, and went to see movies *she* liked—all comedies and romances without a single too-macho hero or blast of machine-gun fire.

She'd felt terrific, like a new woman, like a caged sparrow at last set free.

She'd decided not to work for another advertising agency and tried freelancing instead. Within a few months she'd built up a small but steady clientele and was enjoying herself immensely. She loved being her own boss, reporting to no one, allowing her creative energies to have free reign.

The only problem was money. Business was undependable—too busy one week and quiet the next.

When Bob Dawson called from San Francisco, he'd caught her in a weak moment. She'd just gone over her bank statement. She'd been forced to admit that her earnings barely covered her living expenses, and her savings would be gone in another month.

Bob had seen her design work on a recent, award-winning campaign, and had tracked her down. He'd been so profuse with his compliments that when he asked her to come down for an interview, she couldn't say no.

She had to be in South Lake Tahoe for three weeks anyway, to watch over her brother's house. So she'd agreed to stop off in the city to meet Bob at his office on the way.

"Your artwork and design show remarkable versatility," Bob had said at their meeting two days earlier. "I've been looking for someone like you to take over when our creative director leaves next month. We've got an exciting campaign coming up for Cassera's Hotel and Casino, one of our largest accounts, and I'd like you to work on it."

She'd been amazed by the generous salary he'd offered —even more amazed when he'd invited her to the party tonight to meet Ted Lazar, the casino's general manager. It was an excellent professional opportunity, the dream position that she'd been working toward for six long years.

She hadn't liked Bob at first, although she couldn't say why—and then she'd decided she was wrong. He turned out to be polite and charming.

She ought to have accepted the job in a flash. Instead, she'd told him she needed time to think it over.

Why was she hesitating?

People in jeans and ski jackets streamed in through the double glass doors at the casino's nearby side entrance, bringing in laughter, a blast of cold air, and a flurry of snowflakes. Kelli checked her watch again. Nine o'clock.

Bob was an hour late. What could be keeping him? What if he never showed up?

This is ridiculous, Kelli decided. Go on up to the party and let him join you.

She slid off the stool and hurried past the slot-machine area, around the corner to the hotel elevators. A bell announced the impending arrival of the closest elevator and she stopped in front of it. The doors hissed open and she took a purposeful step forward.

At the same instant a man propelled himself out, and they collided with an impact that sent Kelli staggering backward. She uttered a startled cry just as hands grabbed her arms to steady her, and she found herself eye to eye with the lapel of a charcoal-grey suit.

"Excuse me," said a deep voice.

He took a step sideways, away from the elevator and the other departing passengers. She looked up, still numb with surprise, into a face that was handsome even though its dark brows were drawn together in a distracted scowl.

He looked a few years older than she was. Thirty, maybe thirty-two. He had a straight nose, a determined set to his jaw, and a wide mouth that was pressed together in a tight line. His short, dark brown hair gleamed beneath the overhead lights.

The survey took only a fraction of an instant. He stood just inches away, still gripping her arms with his head tilted down to hers, so that despite his height, she couldn't help but stare directly into his eyes. They were a rich, vibrant blue, like the Tahoe sky, surrounded by thick, dark lashes; quick, intelligent eyes, which at this moment sparked with irritation.

Despite this—for some inexplicable reason—she felt a sudden, wild fluttering inside her—a feeling of momentous, impending change.

"Fate," she thought, and realized, too late, that she'd said it out loud.

He released her arms. His scowl vanished and his eyes lit with interest and a surprising warmth. "What?"

She cleared her throat. "Nothing."

"I thought you said fate."

"No, I said ... late."

"Late?"

"I'm ... late," she said. "For a very important ... date."

His lips twitched with amusement. "Curiouser and curiouser."

She realized she'd babbled a line straight out of *Alice's Adventures in Wonderland,* and he'd responded in kind. She blushed.

"I'm sorry I rammed into you. I shouldn't have been in such a hurry."

"My fault." He waved away her apology. "I wasn't in the world's best mood, or I would have watched where—" In a single, rapid glance he took in her formal attire, and a speculative gleam came into his eyes. "You wouldn't by any chance be going to the party upstairs, would you? The one on the top floor?"

"Yes, I am."

"And you're on the list? They're expecting you?"

"I think so."

He rubbed his chin thoughtfully for a moment. "Listen, would you ... " He checked his watch and a perturbed look flitted across his face.

"I know this is an imposition, but can I ask you a favor? I'm supposed to meet someone at that party, but it looks like he forgot to leave my name at the door. No one gets in if they're not on the list, and they've got Attila the Hun guarding the door. I've come up all the way from San Francisco and I'll be damned if I'm going to leave now."

"So, you want me to ... what?" Kelli asked, a spark of excitement surging through her. "Smuggle you in? Pretend you're my date?"

He nodded, his eyes searching her face. "Would you?"

"I don't know. Who are you supposed to meet?"

"Ted Lazar."

"The casino general manager?" The very man Bob wanted her to meet tonight.

He nodded.

"What's it about?"

"Business." He waved his hand impatiently. "It's too complicated to go into. But the timing on this thing is critical, and it's getting late. I want to get in there before Ted decides to take off."

Kelli wondered how much of his story was true. *Business*, he'd said. How vague was *that*? What if he was using her to get inside for some illicit purpose? No, she couldn't believe that. She saw no threat in his anxious, blue gaze. Instinct told her she could trust him. And the element of intrigue ... well, intrigued her.

The elevator touched down again and a handful of

people in party dress spewed out. "Well?" he asked, gesturing toward the waiting lift.

Life is not a spectator sport, Kelli reminded herself. This was the most interesting, attractive man she'd met in years. A smile lit her face.

"Sure. Why not?" She stepped lightly into the empty elevator in front of him.

He punched the button for the top floor. "I can't tell you how much I appreciate this." They began to ascend, and he leaned against the side wall and smiled at her for the first time. He looked even more handsome when he smiled. Disarmingly so.

"What's your name?"

"Kelli Ann Harrison."

"Kelli Ann. Beautiful name. It suits you."

She held on to the side rail, her heart beating oddly as his eyes held hers for a long moment. "Thanks. And you are?"

"Grant Pembroke."

"Hi, Grant."

He said hi back, his gaze never leaving her face. Bemused by his intense study, she dragged her eyes away from his, focusing instead on the collar of his expensive-looking blue shirt.

His suit was beautifully tailored and looked expensive, too. He probably had a desk job. No, something more adventuresome than that. "Are you with the CIA?"

His eyes widened. "The CIA?"

"Well, you know, all this cloak-and-dagger stuff. Very suspicious."

He laughed. It was a low-pitched, pleasant laugh, and

she liked the way it sounded in the enclosed space. "This is hardly cloak and dagger. More like block and tackle."

She wanted to ask him more, but the elevator slowed and jerked to a halt. Another bevy of partygoers waited in the hotel hallway as they squeezed out.

Grant led the way down the ribbon of red-and-black patterned carpet to a small table where a stocky guard in the hotel uniform sat reading a magazine. Kelli could hear the hum of laughter and conversation through the closed door beside him marked Presidential Suite.

"My date finally got here." Grant told the guard Kelli's name. "Check and see if Lazar put her on the list instead of me."

The doorman picked up a sheaf of papers from the table and made a slow, meticulous check mark beside her name.

"This man is with you?" he asked, frowning.

Kelli smiled and nodded. With a shrug, he hauled himself out of his chair and opened the door. Grant accompanied her inside, where a crowd of people in elegant evening dress milled against a backdrop of soft music and drifting cigarette smoke.

Christmas was still three weeks away, but the room, like the rest of the hotel and casino, was alive with tasteful holiday décor. Tantalizing aromas wafted toward her from an elaborate hors d'oeuvres table in the center of the room.

Grant drew her away from the door and leaned close to her ear. "Thanks," he whispered.

His breath was a sweet, moist vapor against skin that seared with unexpected heat.

"You're welcome," she said softly.

He straightened and inclined his head to search through the crowd. His hand still at her back, he said distractedly, "Will you be free later? Because if you are, this won't take long. Would you like to meet back here in say, about an hour?"

Kelli was seized by an impulse to accept, to say as a matter of fact, I'm free for the evening, and I'd love to meet you anywhere, anytime. But reason intervened. Bob *had* invited her, and he'd show up any minute.

"I'm sorry. I can't. I'm meeting someone."

Grant's blue eyes dimmed with apparent regret. "Anyone important?"

"Possibly my boss."

"Possibly your boss?"

"He offered me a position with his company. I haven't accepted it yet."

"I see." He ran a hand through his hair and shook his head with a worried frown. "Still, is this going to get you in trouble? Letting me in like that? The doorman's sure to tell him—"

"Don't worry about it. I'll come up with some excuse."

"I don't know. I'd hate to see—"

"I'll be fine. Honest."

He sighed. "Well, then, so be it." He paused for a couple of heartbeats, looking into her eyes. "Goodbye, Kelli Ann Harrison." He held out his hand.

She placed her hand in his. As she returned his firm handshake, unsteady pulses began to thump in strange places in her body.

"Thanks again," he said.

She had to blink twice to watch him as he turned and

wove his way through the crowd. It wasn't until he'd disappeared from sight that she let out the breath she'd been holding in a long, wistful sigh.

Well. So much for a brush with destiny—the proverbial chance encounter with a mysterious stranger. She had acted spontaneously, lived a bit dangerously, then duty called and *poof!* She was right back where she started.

Normal, everyday existence.

She caught herself. What was wrong with *normal?* Things were shaping up very nicely in her life at the moment, thank you very much. She relished her independence. She wasn't looking for another entangling relationship. She'd barely recovered from the last one. It was just as well that Grant had walked away.

Kelli wandered idly through the room for several minutes, observing the partygoers, mulling over a few possible explanations to give Bob. A tuxedoed waiter offered her a glass of champagne—one of her favorite beverages—but she declined, wanting to keep her head clear for the meeting to come.

Instead, she crossed to the circular buffet table, where a tiered silver centerpiece spilled over with fresh fruit of every color and description. An attractive arrangement of trays below was filled with plump prawns, stuffed mushrooms, puff pastries, and marinated chicken wings. The mingling aromas made her mouth water.

She was about to reach for a plate when a laugh caught her attention. Her eyes shot toward an adjoining room, where among the milling crowd, she saw Grant shaking hands with a rotund man in a dark-blue suit. Lazar? she wondered hopefully.

A giddy sense of elation swept over her, as if she'd just helped perpetrate an undercover scheme of vast magnitude and importance. He couldn't have done it without me, she thought—and then realized she didn't know what *it* was.

Was that fair? Couldn't he at least have told her what business he was in?

She slipped into the next room, squeezed between a knot of people, and stopped behind a leafy potted palm as tall as the door.

I'll just listen long enough to find out why he's here, she promised herself, parting the fronds slightly and peering through at Grant's back a few feet away.

"Don't be too hard on him, Ted," Grant was saying. *Ted. So it was Ted Lazar.* "He was just doing his job."

"Job, shmob. I'm gonna give him hell." Ted was a head shorter than Grant, about the same height as herself, a paternal type with a fringe of white hair and a congenial yet commanding air. "Stupid of me to forget, it's been a hectic day, but he shouldn't have turned you away without looking for me."

"Don't worry about it," Grant said. "I managed to get in." Kelli liked the way his tapered grey suit jacket fit smoothly across the wide expanse of his shoulders and the slope of his back. "I know you're on a tight deadline, so I didn't want to waste any time. I've had my eye on Cassera's for years, Ted. We're the people you're looking for. We can do a hell of a job for you."

"Not so fast, Grant." Ted's laugh was low and gravelly. "I didn't promise anything. I just said we'd talk."

"If you're not happy with the people handling you now, I'd think you'd want to do more than just talk."

"Maybe." Ted lifted a cigar to his lips and inhaled deeply, then squinted puffy eyes and blew out a slow column of smoke. "When you called this morning, I agreed to meet you because I've seen your work. Damned good. One of the best ad agencies in San Francisco, I'm told, even if you're not one of the biggest. And your list of clients is impressive."

Kelli let the palm fronds flip back into place and froze, her heart pounding in sudden comprehension. Grant Pembroke owned an advertising agency. He was here to try to steal the casino account from Bob Dawson!

"Kelli! There you are." A hand touched Kelli's shoulder and she jumped, repressing a startled scream. "I've been looking all over for you," Bob said.

He wore a black suit and striped shirt that looked positively dapper, and his thick silvery-blond mane was carefully combed, not a hair out of place.

"Sorry I'm so late," he continued. "I got tied up at the office and couldn't get away. Then traffic was horrendous —it took me five hours to get here." He elbowed his way back into the main suite, pulling her with him. "The guard told me you came in with someone. Why didn't you tell me you wanted to bring a friend?"

"I ran into him unexpectedly," Kelli said. *That was certainly true, wasn't it?* "He only stayed a few minutes."

"Where did he go? You shouldn't have brought him up here. He wasn't cleared." Bob grabbed two champagne glasses from a passing tray and handed one to Kelli. He raised his glass. "To my newest and most attractive creative director. Cheers." He took a long drink.

I haven't accepted the job yet, Kelli wanted to tell him,

staring dubiously at her glass. Champagne was for celebra-
tions. Weddings. Christenings. Bon-voyage parties.
Romantic evenings for two. Somehow, she didn't feel like
celebrating tonight.

"What do you think about all this?" Bob indicated the
crowded room with a nod of his head. "Did you take a look
around the casino? Ever work on an account this size?" He
took another drink. "Wait till you meet Lazar. He's a sweetheart of a guy. Let's go find him and introduce you."

Kelli tensed with anxiety. "No, wait." Grant would no
doubt be talking to Ted Lazar for a while. What would Bob
say if he discovered *she'd* admitted one of his *competitors* to
the party? Somehow, she had to keep them apart.

"Before I meet him I should know everything that's
going on with the account," she said, trying to stall for
time. "You told me yesterday there's a big campaign
coming up?"

Bob nodded. "*Big* is an understatement. The board
decided they're tired of the old logo and the look we've
been using on all the collateral materials. They want a
brand-new print image for the hotel and casino, everything revamped. And a new campaign to go with it."

Kelli took a surprised breath. Everything revamped. A
hotel and casino this large would use a ton of collateral
materials—brochures, menus, coupons, stationery, rate
cards—not to mention a whole new ad campaign.

"The account's kept us pretty busy for six years. But
we're talking big bucks now."

Kelli felt a rush of excitement. She'd never worked on a
project of such magnitude. Dawson Advertising must not

be on retainer, or Grant wouldn't be here trying to steal the account away. "Is anyone else bidding on this?"

"Just one agency, a small fish out of Reno. Routine stuff, to make sure our prices stay in line. Nothing to worry about."

So, he didn't know about Grant. "Why nothing to worry about?"

"They don't have a chance in hell of coming up with a workable campaign," Bob said with a self-indulgent smirk. "I took a little trip to Reno a few weeks ago. Three of the guy's top people are working for me now—his head account exec, copy chief, and art director. Wasn't hard to spirit them away. Even dedicated souls will move on if you offer them the right price."

His chuckle stopped when he saw the expression on her face. "Don't look so shocked. Everyone does it. It's a cutthroat business. You don't stay on top by sitting back and twiddling your thumbs. You've got to nip trouble in the bud before it starts."

Kelli didn't like where this was heading. Before she could reply, Bob drained his glass and went on:

"Take today, for instance. This hot shot from San Francisco tried to move in on my territory. When Ted told me that he'd called—Ted likes to keep me on my toes, it's a power trip he plays—hell, this account's been mine for six years. I'm not going to waste my time on a proposal of this size while he puts it out to bid to every Tom, Dick, and Harry that comes along. And I'm sure as hell not going to let Pembroke Advertising steal it away."

Kelli's pulse quickened. "What did you do?"

"Just told Ted a few things I 'heard' about Pembroke." Bob chuckled. "Spread a few rumors."

"What did you say?" Kelli asked, her stomach knotting.

"Who cares, as long as it works? Fifty bucks says Ted won't give Grant Pembroke the time of day now."

Kelli felt sick. She'd been uncomfortable in Bob's office the day before, and now she knew why. This man's business tactics turned sleaze into a new art form. How could she have even considered working for him? How could she have considered working for *anyone*?

I may not make much money freelancing, she thought, but at least I have my integrity. She'd only agreed to the interview in a moment of financial despair.

Now she realized she'd never wanted the job in the first place. When she got back to Seattle, she'd build up her business, make a go of it somehow. And she'd never—no, *never*—work for anyone else again.

A weight seemed to lift from her shoulders with this decision, and her gaze slanted back into the adjoining room.

She spotted Grant, still talking to Ted Lazar. Did Grant know Bob was bad-mouthing him behind his back? Someone ought to tell him. She wondered if Ted believed the rumors about Grant, and whether they might ruin Grant's chances to bid on the account.

It would serve Bob right if Grant stole the account out from under his nose, she thought.

"Bob," she said, taking his arm and leading him deeper into the crowd, away from Grant, "I wonder if you'd excuse me for a minute." She glanced meaningfully toward the front door and he nodded in understanding.

"The ladies' lounge is just down the hall," he said, pointing. "Look for me around here when you're through."

"I will." When he'd gone, Kelli made her way back through the crowd into the other room, her heart racing with anticipation. She stopped behind the palm plant again, listening.

"I appreciate you coming up here," Ted said. "The thing is, I don't want to waste your time on this if we're not right for each other. Why don't you call me next week? Give me a few days to check some things out before I give you any details."

"Check what out? Ted, I'll need to get started on this as soon as possible. Let's go down to your office, where it's quiet. Five minutes, that's all I ask."

Ted sighed. "Grant, let me be frank with you. I've heard nothing but praise for the work you do. But quality isn't the only thing I'm looking for. I need performance, someone who can meet my schedule, who's easy to work with. And since I talked to you last, I've heard a few things I don't like. Things that say you don't fit the bill."

"I don't fit the—what are you talking about? Who've you been talking to?"

"I heard you're temperamental," Ted said. "Stubborn. No one wants to work for you. You like to run the whole show. And worse yet, I hear you're slow. You take forever to finish a job."

"That's absurd. I probably have less staff turnover than any agency in the city. We meet our deadlines, Ted, and then some. Ask any one of my clients. I'll give you a list. You can call them tomorrow."

Kelli fumed inwardly. Bob Dawson's nasty rumors were working far too well. She had to do something to help.

Something ....

"I'll make a few calls tomorrow," Ted said. "Maybe I'll talk to someone who'll change my mind. But right now, I don't want to spend any more—"

"Excuse me." Kelli boldly moved forward and stopped at Grant's side. Out of the corner of her eye, she could see him stiffen in surprise. "Don't believe everything you've heard about Grant's temperament." She fixed Lazar with a dazzling smile. "He's not difficult to work with, I promise you. Honestly, he's a pussycat at heart. And as for the company being slow? Ridiculous. Ten minutes in your office and I'll prove otherwise."

Lazar's bushy brows lifted in fatherly admiration. "Is that right? And who are you, little lady?"

Kelli grinned at Grant, who was staring at her in wide-eyed astonishment, then turned back to Lazar and extended her hand. "I'm Kelli Ann Harrison, Creative Director for Pembroke Advertising."

ABOUT THE AUTHOR

SYRIE JAMES is a *USA Today* and international bestselling author of more than a dozen critically acclaimed novels of historical fiction, romance, and young adult fiction that have been published in 21 languages, including *Dracula, My Love* and the #1 Amazon bestselling Victorian historical romance *Duke Darcy's Castle.*

Hailed by Los Angeles Magazine as the "queen of nine-teenth century re-imaginings," Syrie loves to write about strong women and bold heroes whose chemistry is off the chart, and enjoys sending them on challenging journeys of growth and discovery.

A huge fan of All Things English, Syrie's books have

been Library Journal Editor's Picks of the Year (*The Lost Memoirs of Jane Austen* and *Jane Austen's First Love*), received starred reviews from Publisher's Weekly and Kirkus (ie. *The Missing Manuscript of Jane Austen*), and won numerous awards including the Audiobook Audie (*The Secret Diaries of Charlotte Brontë*).

A member of the Writer's Guild of America, Historical Novel Society, and Jane Austen Society of North America, Syrie has sold scripts to film and television and addressed organizations and literary conferences across the U.S., Canada, and in England.

Syrie's work as a playwright has been produced in New York, Los Angeles, and Montreal, and she has taken to the boards herself, appearing many times on stage as Jane Austen.

Syrie lives in Los Angeles a stone's throw from her two sons and their wives, where she enjoys long walks, flower gardens, and spends far too much time at her computer.

To learn more, please visit: syriejames.com.

Sign up to receive Syrie's newsletter for updates about her next release and other bookish treats!

 facebook.com/syriejames
 twitter.com/syriejames
 instagram.com/syriejames

Made in the USA
Las Vegas, NV
29 June 2022

50879707R00155